"I'm not going b

Damn! It was his own fault, Loucan realized. He'd declared himself way too soon. "I'm not looking for any kind of decision right away, Lass," he said calmly.

"Well, you're getting one!" Her green eyes blazed and her full lower lip jutted angrily. "My decision is made. I'm not going back to Pacifica. I want you to leave."

"This isn't over, Lass."

"Is that a threat? Are you planning to kidnap me?"

Loucan's jaw tightened in frustration. Kidnap her? What a good idea. "Yes, Lass," he said through clenched teeth, "if I have to."

A Tale of the Sea

MORE THAN MEETS THE EYE by *Carla Cassidy*
IN DEEP WATERS by *Melissa McClone*
CAUGHT BY SURPRISE by *Sandra Paul*
FOR THE TAKING by *Lilian Darcy*

Dear Reader,

What makes readers love Silhouette Romance? Fans who have sent mail and participated on our www.eHarlequin.com community bulletin boards say they enjoy the heart-thumping emotion, the noble strength of the heroines, the truly heroic nature of the men—all in a quick yet satisfying read. I couldn't have said it better!

This month we have some fantastic series for you. Bestselling author Lindsay McKenna visits use with *The Will To Love* (SR 1618), the latest in her thrilling cross-line adventure MORGAN'S MERCENARIES: ULTIMATE RESCUE. Jodi O'Donnell treats us with her BRIDGEWATER BACHELORS title, *The Rancher's Promise* (SR 1619), about sworn family enemies who fight the dangerous attraction sizzling between them.

You must pick up *For the Taking* (SR 1620) by Lilian Darcy. In this A TALE OF THE SEA, the last of the lost royal siblings comes home. And if that isn't dramatic enough, in Valerie Parv's *Crowns and a Cradle* (SR 1621), part of THE CARRAMER LEGACY, a struggling single mom discovers she's a princess!

Finishing off the month are Myrna Mackenzie's *The Billionaire's Bargain* (SR 1622)—the second book in the latest WEDDING AUCTION series—about a most tempting purchase. And *The Sheriff's 6-Year-Old Secret* (SR 1623) is Donna Clayton's tearjerker.

I hope you enjoy this month's selection. Be sure to drop us a line or visit our Web site to let us know what we're doing right—and any particular favorite topics you want to revisit. Happy reading!

Mary-Theresa Hussey

Mary-Theresa Hussey
Senior Editor

Please address questions and book requests to:
Silhouette Reader Service
U.S.: 3010 Walden Ave., P.O. Box 1325, Buffalo, NY 14269
Canadian: P.O. Box 609, Fort Erie, Ont. L2A 5X3

For the Taking

LILIAN DARCY

SILHOUETTE Romance®
Published by Silhouette Books
America's Publisher of Contemporary Romance

Special thanks and acknowledgment are given to Lilian Darcy for her contribution to the A TALE OF THE SEA series.

SILHOUETTE BOOKS

ISBN 0-373-19620-2

FOR THE TAKING

This edition published by arrangement with Harlequin Books S.A.

Visit Silhouette at www.eHarlequin.com

Printed in U.S.A.

Books by Lilian Darcy

Silhouette Romance

The Baby Bond #1390
Her Sister's Child #1449
Raising Baby Jane #1478
**Cinderella After Midnight* #1542
**Saving Cinderella* #1555
**Finding Her Prince* #1567
Pregnant and Protected #1603
For the Taking #1620

*The Cinderella Conspiracy

LILIAN DARCY

has written nearly fifty books for Silhouette Romance and Harlequin Mills & Boon Medical Romance (Prescription Romance). Her first book for Silhouette appeared on the Waldenbooks Series Romance bestsellers list, and she's hoping readers go on responding strongly to her work. Happily married with four active children and a very patient cat, she enjoys keeping busy and could probably fill several more lifetimes with the things she likes to do—including cooking, gardening, quilting, drawing and traveling. She currently lives in Australia, but travels to the United States as often as possible to visit family. Lilian loves to hear from readers. You can write to her at P.O. Box 381, Hackensack, NJ 07602 or e-mail her at lildarcy@austarmetro.com.au.

A TALE OF THE SEA

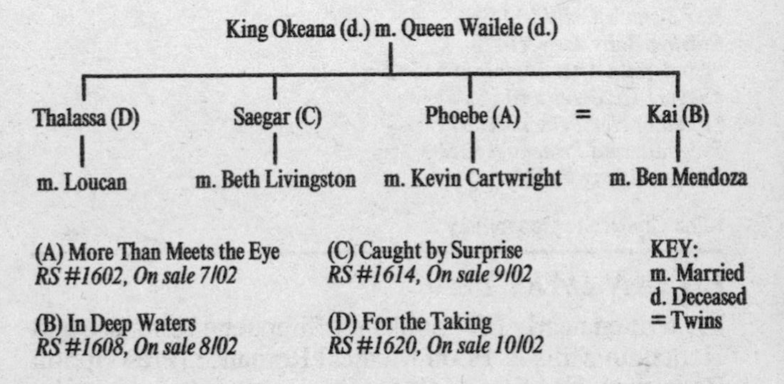

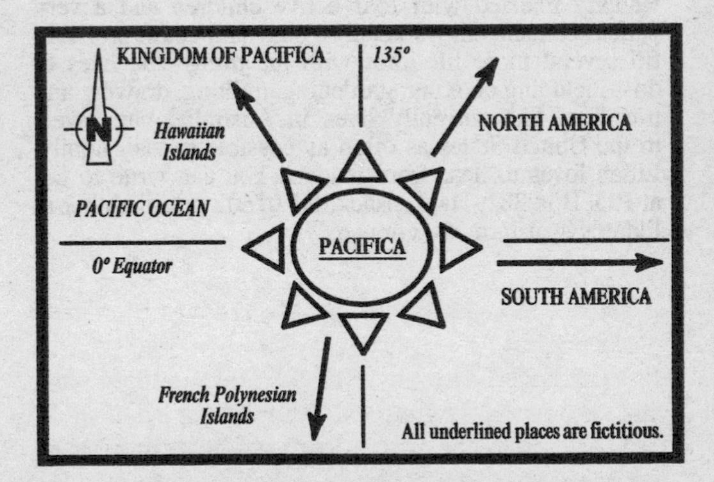

Prologue

This time they met in a bar.

Loucan was at home in places like this. He'd worked in one, a long time ago, for about six months. The yeasty tang of beer in the air was familiar, and the other drinkers didn't think there was anything strange about two men sitting hunched over their filled glasses in the darkest corner of the establishment, locked in conversation.

"So, how is married life?" he asked Kevin Cartwright. It sounded like a casual question, but it wasn't.

"Uh, you know, it's okay," the big man answered. "It's not bad."

Yeah, right! The guy was actually *wrestling* with his uncontrollable grin, and the grin was winning. It just wouldn't stay off his face, no matter how hard he tried. Marriage to Phoebe Jones was clearly a lot better than "not bad."

"I've brought some wedding pictures, if you want to see them," Kevin added.

Loucan didn't waste any time. Ignoring the mention of such a trivial thing as wedding pictures, he pounced at once. "Because I get the impression it's too much of a distraction," he said. "What progress have you made in locating Thalassa since your marriage?"

Kevin sat up straight, gulped some beer and swore. "Where is this coming from, Loucan?" he demanded. "I thought we were here to celebrate three successes, not fling accusations about one failure."

Loucan ignored him. "Have you narrowed down the search?" he asked. "You've been working on this for four years, on and off. Phoebe, Kai and Saegar have all been found. Yes, that's success, but it doesn't mean anything without Lass. She's your sole focus now. I need results, and I have to wonder, is wedded bliss with Phoebe taking the edge off your hunger to close this case?"

"Easy, Loucan...!" Kevin slumped back in his chair. He shook his head slowly several times as he swirled the beer in his glass.

Loucan wasn't fooled by the apparently relaxed posture. They were both strong men. Direct. Sure of themselves. He'd gone on the attack with the deliberate aim of getting the straightest possible answers from the man he'd hired to track down the four far-flung Pacifican royal siblings.

Kevin didn't disappoint him. Leaning forward again with new energy, he took another long gulp of beer, fixed his deep blue eyes on Loucan and said, "Okay. You want the truth? The only thing that finding the other three has done is made me face facts."

"What facts?" Loucan said. "I'm interested in facts. I like them."

"Loucan, we have nothing left to go on. There weren't many avenues to pursue to begin with, and those turned into dead ends real fast. Thalassa and Cyria are both unusual names, but I ran searches through every database and archive I could think of in two hemispheres, and the handful of hits I turned up didn't pan out. Australia and New Zealand, where you think they're located, both have small populations compared to the United States, but that didn't seem to help. I've told you all this."

"Tell me again. Tell me what point you're at now."

"I'm guessing Cyria changed her name, and maybe Lass's as well. I'm guessing she got them each forged identity documents—birth certificates—through some South Pacific nation where bribes get results. We found the other three mainly through luck. Now it seems like our luck has run out."

"You're throwing in the towel?" Loucan felt his scalp tighten with anger. "Giving up the search? This *is* because of Phoebe!"

"It's not," Kevin insisted. "And I'm not throwing it in. I've got one thing left to suggest, the only thing I believe can get a result."

"Yeah? Then I want to hear it. Straight."

"You knew Thalassa," Kevin said. "How old was she when you left Pacifica that first time?

Loucan shrugged impatiently. "That was twenty-five years ago. She was eight and I was fourteen. What does that have to do with anything?"

"You knew her then," Kevin repeated. "And you knew Cyria, who was her guardian. And whatever has happened to both of them since, there are ways in which people don't change. Think, Loucan!" It wasn't quite a command, yet much more than a plea. "You're the one with something to go on. Memories. Impressions. Things you couldn't communicate to me even if you tried, because you're not going to realize what's significant until you're actually living the search."

"Me? Living the search? You want *me* to find her?"

"Yes. If anyone can find Thalassa after all this time, it's you."

Kevin's eyes blazed intently, and he'd balled one hand into a fist. Given the kind of man Kevin Cartwright was, that meant the idea deserved at least Loucan's consideration.

He nodded slowly and narrowed his eyes, thinking, *struggling....*

Memories? Impressions? Lord, it was hard! He'd last seen Thalassa twenty-five years ago, back in Pacifica, when he was just a boy. Since then, he'd had adventures enough for three lifetimes.

He'd spent ten years, and more, roaming the world. He'd swum with pods of whales on their great migrations around the Pacific rim, until he knew every current in that vast ocean. Living on land, he'd worked as a commercial fisherman, an Arizona ranch hand and a Wall Street bond trader. He'd swapped identities easily, and he had hungrily absorbed knowledge and understanding from every experience.

He'd never done anything seriously illegal, but he had been in prison once for several days, arrested by mistake. He'd even been married. That wasn't a memory he liked to dwell on, since it carried with it so much guilt and grief.

For the past fifteen years, he'd spent most of his time in Pacifica, relearning its ways, working to bring together the two warring factions that had divided the mer people for a generation.

But before all of that…

Yes, he realized. He still had memories. One in particular flooded into his mind as he sat and thought, his beer untouched on the table in front of him.

His parents and Thalassa's had been friends once, before Lass's father, King Okeana, had come under the malign influence of an evil, manipulative merman named Joran, and his dangerous ideas. The friendship had already begun to fracture by the time Loucan reached his teens, but the two women, Okeana's wife, Wailele, and Loucan's own mother, Ondina, were still managing to hold it together, the way women sometimes did. There had been no open rift, and no violence, as yet.

The two families had left the safe confines of Pacifica's underwater world and gone on a picnic together, at a secret coral island beach. Around a closed fire made from phosphorus distilled out of the ocean itself, they'd feasted on freshly cooked marine delicacies as well as the exotic and expensive treats of earth-grown foods—bananas, coconuts and baked yams.

Loucan remembered Wailele's frailty. She'd never fully recovered from the difficult birth of the twins, Phoebe and Kai, and could take little part in the day-to-day rearing of her children, particularly lively Lass. Cyria, he remembered, was the dominant influence in Lass's life even then. He remembered her doting strictness. *He* wouldn't have put up with it, he'd thought at fourteen. He remembered Cyria's unwillingness to share Thalassa with others, and her pride in the bright, pretty child.

Take Lass's long, rippling, red-gold hair, for example. It had never been cut.

"And never will, while I have breath in my body!" Cyria had declared in his hearing. "It's far too beautiful, and it sets her apart, as a princess should be."

Lass had seemed unconcerned by Cyria's attitude back then. She had delighted in playing with her toddling sisters, entertaining them by building sand castles and digging holes for the sea to fill.

She'd casually obeyed Cyria's order, "Braid your hair! Keep it out of the sand!" then had gone back to her sisters, with a laugh and a kiss for each of them. She'd made herself a frivolous pair of "shoes" out of shells and strips of seaweed, and all three sisters had giggled as she pranced around in them on the beach. She'd been so full of life and happiness.

But what might have changed since? Cyria and Lass had left Pacifica together, just the two of them, and Cyria's influence could only have grown stronger.

Still, Lass's spirit would have been hard to break. Loucan remembered how she'd left the beach and swum far out into the ocean, lazing there during the minutes it took for her tail membrane to form. He had followed her at a distance, unwillingly impressed by her boldness. She was only a little kid!

Then some dolphins had swum past and she'd joined them, surfing and frolicking in the waves....

Yes, Kevin was right. There were memories.

Kevin was watching him. And watching his untouched beer. Loucan blinked and quirked his lips in a reluctant and self-conscious smile. His voice came out slightly husky as he told the younger man, "I see what you mean. You're right. Maybe I *am* the only one who has a chance of finding her."

And with Kevin's thoughtful and curious gaze still fixed on him, Loucan was struck by a sudden intuition that, after all, finding Thalassa was going to be the easy part.

Chapter One

Thalassa came toward Loucan across a lush field of green grass, where several sleek and well-fed horses grazed.

Her red-gold hair, which still shocked him with its almost boyish length, glinted like polished copper. A clingy, cream knit tank top showed off smooth pale skin and a figure that was just as shapely above the waist as it was below. Her legs were neat and athletic in a pair of khaki stretch pants, and she had brown leather boots on her feet, making her walk easy and confident. She was as graceful and sure in her body as one of the horses she'd just been tending.

Something stirred inside Loucan, and he recognized the feeling with ease. He'd felt it the other night, too—the night they'd first met. He could be attracted to this woman. Very easily. There was something so lush and physical about her. The rich color of her hair. The fullness of her breasts.

There was something very contained and self-sufficient in her emotional makeup, as well. He suspected she wouldn't open up to him easily. She had reasons for that—reasons to do with the past. She'd probably trained herself to be mistrustful.

But it wasn't just a matter of history, of discordant beliefs and opposing factions. It went deeper than that, to the very heart of her. The powerful sensuality he detected in her seemed dormant, as if she hadn't yet discovered it.

Or as if she feared it, and kept it hidden.

As soon as Lass registered his presence on her land, the whole aura of her body changed. She tensed and lifted a hand to shield her eyes against the Australian summer sunlight, which was strong even at nine in the morning.

Yes, she'd recognized him, and she wasn't surprised. Loucan had told her on the beach the other night that he would give her two days—time in which to think, to get used to this, to understand that he wasn't a part of the violence of the past—and then he would come looking for her. In the end, he'd given her three days, but now, as promised, he was here.

She wouldn't even acknowledge him at first. They were still some distance apart. He leaned against the side of his dark blue rental car and took in the details of her place, while she swung two feed buckets in her hands and scowled up at the leafy tops of the eucalyptus trees, moving in a light breeze.

Lass had found a pretty incredible home for herself, Loucan decided. At the end of a gravel path lined with nasturtiums and lavender stood a quaint old building with a veneer of pale yellow stucco and a mantle of leafy green wisteria.

According to an elegantly carved and painted sign,

this was The Old Dairy—Tearoom and Gallery. The sign listed its opening hours, as well as the fact that "light meals and Devonshire teas" were served. Lass owned the place, and the land it was situated on. Several acres, if he was judging it right.

Beyond the tearoom building, and connected to it by another path, was a low, gracious house built in the Australian colonial style, with a galvanized metal roof that curved down to form what Loucan now knew was called a bull-nosed veranda.

At the moment, the veranda was filled with morning sunshine. It made the terra-cotta pots of bright flowers stand out like beacons. Later, though, as the day grew hot, the long sweep of stone flagging would be darkened by cool shade.

Behind the house was a stable and a shed or two, neatly kept, then more green fields and forest, and finally, in the distance, the mountains. Wild mountains, Loucan observed, clothed in forests of sage-green eucalyptus.

This view to the west was impressive enough, but behind Loucan, in the opposite direction, it was even better. More significant, too. It told him much more about Lass than she probably wanted him to know. About three miles away, beyond lush dairy country, beyond a scattering of small towns, beyond tidal lakes, rocky headlands and miles of pristine sandy beaches, was the beckoning sea.

Technically, it was the Tasman Sea, this two-thousand-mile stretch between the coasts of Australia and New Zealand, but in reality it was an integral part of the Pacific Ocean. It stretched, blue and sparkling, in a long, wide ribbon from north to south, and in the summer haze its horizon blurred indistinctly with the almost garishly blue sky. The whole scene was breathtaking.

"You came," Lass said.

He turned to find her watching him from a distance of twenty feet or so. "I said I would."

"I hoped you wouldn't. I didn't want to see you again."

"I know."

He had a sudden flashback to the other night's most shocking moment. After he had told her who he was and how he had found her, she had fled from him across the sand in the darkness to hide among the jagged piles of rocks on the nearby headland. He had followed her, and found her sobbing wildly, in anger and fear, while hacking at her gorgeous fall of hair—it reached to her thighs—with a jagged piece of oyster shell.

"I like your hair that way," he said to her now. He wasn't going to let her avoid the difficult issues between them. He couldn't pretend. They both needed to confront this.

"I'm getting used to it," she answered guardedly. Self-conscious, she ran her fingers through its short, bright strands, making it seem more alive than ever. The gesture momentarily deepened the cleft between her breasts and drew his gaze. "I went to my hairdresser on Wednesday morning to get it properly shaped," she added.

"What did you tell her?"

She shrugged. "That I'd grown sick of it, suddenly. That it was too much work, so I'd chopped it off."

She was so prickly and distant and defensive! Loucan knew how emotional she had been the other night when he'd found her on the beach and told her who he was, but she was trying to pretend her outburst had never happened.

"Why did you hack it off like that?" he persisted.

"You know why."

Yes, but I want to hear it from your own mouth.

She had a passionate mouth, he observed. It was full-lipped, sensuous and strong. With a surge of understanding, he gave in and said it for her. "Because your hair was the thing that led me to you."

Her nod was just a brief jerk of her jutting chin, and her green eyes were narrowed.

"Does this mean you're going to hurt the dolphins, too?" He asked, then ignored her shocked hiss of breath. "Hearing that you'd been seen surfing with them at sunset was what clinched it for me. I knew you were the woman I'd been looking for, and I knew where to find you."

"Hurt the—!" She shook her head and swallowed, outraged.

Maybe he'd gone too far. He wanted to push her into talking about what she believed and why she was so scared, but this wasn't the way. She wasn't like Kevin Cartwright, who rose to the bait of a direct attack. She was a woman—a mer woman, if she could accept that—and therefore very different.

He was about to apologize, but she hadn't stopped speaking. "Why are you doing this? I won't tolerate it. Leave my property, please!"

She turned in the direction of the house, ignoring him as he followed her. When she reached the veranda, she clumsily levered off her elastic-sided riding boots and socks, and tossed them into a basket beside the door. Retrieving a pair of flimsy, high-heeled cream sandals from the same basket, she slipped them onto her feet and tottered inside.

Still he followed her. Still she ignored him. It would get to be a habit between them, soon. Almost immediately, as if hardly noticing what she'd done, she kicked the sandals off again and frowned down at her pink manicured toes.

Did she have a love-hate relationship with her footwear? Or with her feet?

She tipped her head to one side thoughtfully and said, "Is it enough to tell you that I'm busy this morning? Or should I phone the police?"

"Thalassa—"

"My name is Lass. Or Letitia Susan Morgan, if you want the full, legal version."

"Cyria did change your name, then."

"Who? Oh, you mean Aunt Catherine?"

"Do I?" His gaze held hers for a moment, and it was a toss-up whose was the most stubborn. He changed tack. "You have a fabulous view of the ocean, Lass."

"I prefer the view in the other direction. To the mountains."

"No, you don't," he told her softly. "It's not the mountains you watch. It's not the mountains that call you. You couldn't stay away, could you? You couldn't when you bought this place, and you still can't."

She lifted her chin, and he appreciated the stubborn yet delicate line of her jaw. "I go for weeks, sometimes, without setting foot on the beach."

He laughed. "You sound like a gambler, talking about visits to the track. You do without it for weeks, but you think about it every day. Are you really going to call the police?''

''Yes! And I really don't have time to talk! The tearoom opens at ten, and there's a ton of stuff to do to prepare. My staff will be here any minute.''

''I have something for you from your sisters, Lass.''

Loucan didn't wait for another defensive answer, another threat to throw him off the property. He just reached into the breast pocket of his conservative and anonymous navy T-shirt and pulled out a paper packet.

''Wedding pictures,'' he said, and took the sheaf of prints out of the packet to show her. He knew exactly what effect it would have. It was his one asset in all this, and he was counting on it.

Watching her reaction, he saw that he wasn't wrong.

Lass gasped and clamped a fist to her heart. Pictures? Of Phoebe and Kai? She had long ago shut off any hope of finding them, had often wondered if they were even still alive. She had thought of trying to trace them somehow, but it had seemed like such a hopeless quest. She didn't even know to which part of the world or with whom her father had sent them. Didn't know if they were together or apart.

She hadn't seen them since they were two years old. They'd been the light of her life, back then—the beings she'd loved most in the world. She still remembered the soft, plump feel of their little cheeks pressed against hers for a ''Tiss, Lassie. I want a tiss!'' She remembered the exuberant embrace of their little arms, the innocent joyousness of their laughter and the equal intensity of their tears. And now they were grown women, old enough to be married.

She wanted to hear about her sisters.

Set against this longing, all her bravado toward Loucan was fake. For the sake of her sisters, she would make herself believe what he said—that he hadn't been part of the violence. Because of her sisters, she wouldn't turn him off her property.

And he knew it, too. Oh, he knew it.

He'd brought those pictures with him on purpose, and he'd mentioned them at exactly the right moment. Now he was cradling them closely in his hand. On the surface, it was a casual gesture, but she knew he was doing it with deliberate intent. She wasn't going to get to touch those pictures until he chose to let her, and since they were so precious to her, she didn't dare try and grab them from him by force.

Against a man like Loucan, she would have no hope of success. His strength had been apparent to her from the beginning. It wasn't just about his powerful size or his almost intimidating good looks. There was an unusual force of will displayed in those incredible blue eyes. This man knew what he wanted.

His thick, dark hair was pulled into a short, tight braid that lay against the back of his neck, making him look like an English sailor from two hundred years ago. The style revealed the regal height and breadth of his forehead and emphasized his square jaw and very masculine bone structure.

He'd frightened her on the beach the other night, from the moment his strong, deep voice had uttered her name. Her full, real name. No one had used it since Cyria died.

Thalassa.

It meant "one who comes from the sea."

She shivered a little, and wished she was wearing something more substantial than this snug top this morning. She felt vulnerable, physically and emotionally, but wasn't going to let it show if she could possibly help it.

"Show me the photos!" she demanded.

In his hand she caught the tiniest glimpse of a gorgeous couple dressed in wedding finery, and her heart did a flip against her rib cage. Was that lovely woman with the honey-colored hair Phoebe? Or was it Kai? Oh lord, she should *know!* A woman should be able to recognize her own sisters!

The phone rang—so perfectly timed that she almost suspected Loucan of engineering the call somehow.

She was tempted to let it ring, except that when you ran a small business essentially on your own, you couldn't afford to do that. All her calls were potentially important. In any case, Loucan had taken advantage of the moment and had hidden the photos back in their packet.

"Take the call," he said. "This can wait."

She was already running to the phone that was fixed to the kitchen wall. It was her decision to take the call, not his! She *refused* to respond to his arrogant orders, and she wasn't going to let him underestimate her.

"Lass?" The voice on the other end of the line was shaky, but she recognized it right away.

"Susie? What's up?"

"We've just had an accident. Rob was driving, but it wasn't his fault...."

"Oh, Lord, Susie, are you all okay?"

Susie and her sister Megan helped in the tearoom

kitchen every day, while Susie's husband, Rob, came part-time to keep the garden in shape and handle maintenance. Susie and Rob were in their late twenties, hoping to start a family soon, and Lass was close to them.

Well, as close as she ever let herself get to anybody.

"We're fine." Susie burst into tears.

They were obviously not fine. In a rambling account, Lass heard the details. Susie had lacerations on her face, Megan was being assessed for a head injury and Rob had probably broken something, but they weren't yet sure what. They were at the emergency department of the local hospital.

"I'll try to get out to you as soon as I can," Susie promised, "but they want to put dressings on the cuts, and—"

"Susie, you're not coming in today, okay? None of you. Or tomorrow. Not till you're ready. It should be quiet. I'll—"

"Quiet? It's the middle of school summer break!"

"I'll manage. We can still get quiet days sometimes. You just look after yourself and Megan and Rob."

The fact that Susie stopped arguing at once was proof that neither she, her sister nor Rob were fit to come in. Lass put down the phone, and faced the knowledge that "managing" wouldn't be nearly as easy as she'd claimed. She opened in less than an hour, and still had the salads and sandwich ingredients to set out, the quiche fillings to prepare, the coffee machine to start, the scones to make, the cream to whip....

And she didn't care.

"Show me the photos, Loucan."

Coming through the doorway from the kitchen, her bare feet cool on the polished hardwood floor, she found him standing in front of one of the two sets of French doors that opened onto the veranda, in the direction of the sea.

He was watching the sparkling blue ocean, just the way she always did. Silent, still and totally absorbed. Hungry for it. Listening to its call.

But he couldn't hate the power of that call, the way she did.

He turned at her words, and he wasn't holding the photos anymore. Where had he hidden them? She couldn't tell. Not in the T-shirt pocket.

"I heard your conversation," he said. "Your help can't make it today?"

She shrugged. "It's okay. I'm worried about them, not me. It seems as if none of them is seriously hurt, fortunately. Please show me the photos of Phoebe and Kai. And—and Saegar, too." The brother and playmate she'd loved. "Do you have pictures of him?"

"No, I'm sorry. I don't."

"News about him, then? You told me the other day you were in touch with him."

"You didn't believe me."

"I do now. Tell me. Show me."

"Not yet. Tell me what's in it for me, first, Thalassa." His blue eyes burned with a cool fire, an assessing look she didn't trust. "Meet me halfway. If I give you what you want, will you listen to me? Will you give me—?"

"No!" she cried, pressing her palms to her ears. "How can you talk about giving? Your father and his supporters took from me something that can never be replaced. They took my mother's life with unspeakable violence, and without warning.'' She drew a shuddery breath and had to struggle to keep going. ''I'm giving you nothing, Loucan!''

As always, when she thought about her mother's death, she couldn't fight the secret, nightmare memory. Cyria—she'd only ever called her guardian Aunt Catherine in public—was the only other person who knew what Lass had witnessed as an eight-year-old child, and now Cyria was dead, too. That death, at least, had been peaceful.

Her mother's, Wailele's, wasn't.

Oh, dear God, must I see it in my memory for the rest of my life?

Still, after twenty-five years, the sight of blood in the water panicked and terrified her, and she had told Cyria time and again that she would never go back to Pacifica, where such violence might happen once more.

''Then I guess the photos aren't needed today,'' Loucan said, cutting across her relentless unfolding of memory. He still seemed cool and totally in control.

''How do I even know they're genuine?'' she argued. ''I haven't seen Phoebe or Kai in so long, those couples could be anyone.'' She didn't really believe that. She knew in her heart that they were Phoebe and Kai, and their new husbands. All the same… ''I don't trust you, Loucan!''

''That's obvious,'' he said. ''And I can understand it.''

''I hope so!''

''What I can't understand is that you'd deny yourself the chance to connect with your brother and your sisters purely because you don't want to have anything to do with me."

"Not so surprising, if you'd think about it a little more." Deliberately, she kept her voice hard. "You're apparently willing to blackmail me by keeping me in ignorance of the only family I have left. What that says about your character doesn't inspire me to get to know you any better. But you've given me some facts about Phoebe and Kai and Saegar. Where they're living. The names they use. I'll be patient."

"You're saying—"

"Yes. I'll track them down myself, or I'll employ someone to do it. I don't need you, Loucan. Your blackmail attempt has failed. And now I need to open up the tearoom. You can let yourself out."

She slipped her feet into her sandals, pulled a bunch of keys from her pocket and opened the door, quaking inside. What would he do? Would he call her bluff? Could she bear it if he gave up and left, without telling her more about her siblings and without showing her the photos? Would the facts she now had be enough to trace her family on her own, as she'd suggested?

The heels of her silly, impractical shoes rapped like gunshots on the stone flagging of the veranda. Why did she buy these things? She had a dozen pairs and they killed her feet all day. Her clientele wouldn't raise their eyebrows if she wore flats. Half the time she kicked her shoes off behind the counter and didn't even notice.

She felt her breasts bounce as she clicked along to the end of the veranda, and was self-conscious again, aware of her own body in a way that was unusual.

She didn't like to think about where Loucan's gaze might be focused.

He was a powerful man. Powerful in his position at the center of the chaotic situation that apparently still existed in Pacifica. Powerful in the aura of determination and ruthlessness that he exuded. He hadn't given up. He would call her bluff; she was sure of it. Was he watching? Why didn't he say something?

Loucan didn't find his voice until Lass had reached the end of the veranda. He couldn't understand his own reluctance to speak. She wouldn't carry through on her threat, he was sure.

And yet he heard himself saying, with a husky note in his strong voice, "Wait!"

"Yes?" She turned, and he saw that he'd been right. She wasn't remotely cool about this. He saw her hands shaking and her eyes glittering with hot tears.

"I'm not going to blackmail you." He spread his hands in a gesture of helplessness that he couldn't remember ever using before in his life. "And I was wrong to imply that I would. I want your alliance and your trust, not this."

"Sure you do, Loucan." She pivoted and stepped from the veranda onto the paved path that led to the tearoom.

"Lass, listen to me—"

"No!"

He followed her, faster than she was in those frivolous, kittenish heels. Hearing him gaining on her, she kicked them off once more, and abandoned them in the grass at the side of the path. He caught up to her anyway, grasped her shoulder and spun her around. He pinned her to the spot with the sheer force of his will.

"This is how wars start," he said urgently. "This is where violence comes from. When people can't find a way to talk."

She lifted that strong, stubborn chin. "Is that what happened in Pacifica, all those years ago? Not as far as I'm concerned!"

"You were too young to understand. If you'd listen to me, I could tell you. My father had nothing to do with your mother's death."

"Oh, he didn't?"

"No. He was horrified that one of his supporters had taken a speech of his and interpreted it in that way. The man was acting totally alone."

He heard the smallest tremor of doubt in his own voice, and wondered if Lass had picked up on it. He still wasn't sure of the whole truth himself. There was a tiny thread of evidence—the report of one witness—that suggested Joran, one of Okeana's own supporters, had incited the fanatical assassin to murder Okeana's wife in order to further the unrest that Joran sought.

For the moment, however, Loucan ignored the possibility. It was a detail that didn't affect his own innocence. He had been three thousand miles from Pacifica when Wailele died.

He pressed on.

"Listen to me, Lass. Trust me at least long enough for us to talk about Phoebe and Kai and Saegar, and for me to tell you why I'm here. I'm not just looking for your belief in my version of the past. There's more than that. I've spent years searching for you. Give me some time. Let me help you in the tearoom today, and we'll—"

She laughed. "You? The self-styled rightful king of Pacifica, Loucan the Triumphant, or whatever you've decided to call yourself, cutting tomatoes and stacking the dishwasher? What could your royal majesty possibly know about my kitchen?"

He grinned, seeing the chance to soften her with humor, and grabbing it.

"I admit I'm more experienced at tending bar than pouring coffee," he said, still smiling as he invited her to share his amusement. "But I've worked in the galley of a commercial fishing boat, cooking a hot breakfast for twelve hungry men after we've been up all night hauling nets. I know which side of a teapot to hold, and which to pour from."

"Big deal!"

"I bussed tables once for a few months, a long time ago, when I was around seventeen. You should see how fast I can flick a wet cloth around, when it's needed. You need help today, and I'm offering. For less than minimum wage. Couldn't we start from there?"

His smile was as hot as summer sunlight and as powerful as the sea itself. It pulled at Lass's emotions, the way the ocean did in all its moods.

Loucan knew all about that. He was a creature of the ocean himself. Even so, she would have forced herself to stay immune to his smile if he hadn't pulled the packet of photos from the tight back pocket of his jeans, and added casually, "Tell me what to do to start setting up, and you can look at these while I work."

"All right. Okay. Uh...I'm not— This isn't a capitulation, Loucan," she insisted. "All it is...it's for Saegar and my sisters."

"I know that," he said quietly. "I understand. By the end of the day, I hope your reasons will change, but for now it's good enough."

"Okay," she said again. The word hardly had meaning. "Good."

Unlocking the door that opened directly into the gallery, she led the way past blue-green seascapes, glazed ceramics and trays of delicate jewelry, feeling as if she was walking with Loucan into a new future she hadn't even imagined three days ago. She was terrified of everything about it.

Chapter Two

Cyria was the one who had taught her to be afraid, and to set herself apart.

Time and again, she had held Lass close to her and whispered, "No one should have to see what you've seen. We'll never go back. Not unless your father himself comes to claim you and tells us that Pacifica is safe for us again. Promise me that."

"I promise, Cyria. Only if it's safe."

As Lass grew older, she heard the same message from Cyria in more sophisticated language.

"We'll stay hidden here," Cyria said. "Forever, if we have to. King Okeana will come for us only if it's safe. If we're careful, no one will suspect that we are mer. These land-dwellers, they have no soul and no sense. It would never occur to them that all their silly legends about mer people could possibly contain an element of truth. Joran was right in what he told your father. We must use our kinship with the land-dwellers to take what we need from them, but we must never make the mistake of thinking they are our equals. *You* in particular, Thalassa. You are a mer princess, and you must never forget it."

Of course, Lass hadn't blindly accepted everything Cyria told her. Young girls didn't, particularly once they reached the adolescent years of rebellion and quest for selfhood. But enough of it had stuck, enough had grafted itself to her nature and helped to form the woman she now was.

When she swam, she did so secretly, and almost always after dark, because she never knew exactly how long it would take for her tail membrane to form. She'd had no one to tutor her in the chemistry and physiology of the process, and had worked out a hazy understanding of it by herself, through trial and error.

It was quicker at the full moon. Slower when the water was cold. Something to do with the sea's saltiness, too, because it always took longer to happen when she swam near the mouth of the tidal lake next to her favorite beach, where a freshwater stream emptied into the sea.

If Cyria knew the science of it, she hadn't passed on the knowledge. She had forbidden Lass to swim in the ocean at all.

"You could be killed as if you were a fish, before you could even cry out, if anyone saw your tail. Or you could be captured and tortured in the name of science."

Lass had tried to argue at first. It would be perfectly safe to take a short swim, even in broad daylight, as long as she left the water in time. Her tail membrane did not even begin to form for at least fifteen minutes.

But Cyria wouldn't hear of it, so Lass swam guiltily as well as secretly. She'd been doing it since the age of fourteen, but there had been defiance rather than guilt in the act until she was twenty. The guilt came after Cyria's death. The old woman had worked so hard and sacrificed so much for Lass's safety. She'd sincerely believed that the ocean was too dangerous.

"But I can't give it up. I *can't!*" Lass had told herself, over and over, in the first acute days of mourning her guardian's loss. "I'll do everything else Cyria wanted. I'll keep my hair. I'll run a business that's under my own control and where there's never anyone I have to get too close to. She's right. Friendships are dangerous. Ondina and my mother thought that their friendship was enough to keep peace in Pacifica, and they were wrong. And I'll never fall in love with a land-dwelling man."

She'd already had proof that Cyria was right in that area. She'd had a boyfriend at college who'd taken her out several times and then told her, just as she was beginning to let down her guard, "There's something weird about you. I don't think I want to go on with this. I'm sorry." She hadn't accepted any dates after that, and after a while, word got around and no one asked.

"I'll never have a child, who could turn out to be mer. But I have to swim…sometimes. Not too often. Or I might as well just die…."

Even so, she kept trying to give it up. She learned to love horseback riding and hiking in the wild Australian bush country. She told herself that eventually she would wean herself away from the sea.

But she couldn't. She just couldn't. And so Loucan, son of her father's enemy, had found her….

* * *

Summer was the most dangerous time of year—the season when Lass tried hardest, and failed most often, to stay away. The water was at its warmest, so her tail formed faster. The beaches were more crowded, so she had to be watchful and seek the most isolated places.

Lass hadn't been to the ocean for weeks—not since the start of school summer vacation in mid-December. And now Christmas and New Year had passed, and it was late January.

And she was ready to snap. She *had* snapped. Three times today, at Susie and Megan, over trivialities. That was out of character. Normally, she didn't have a flashing temper, and in any case she'd found long ago that a cheerful attitude toward others invited less curiosity, and fewer questions.

Today, she knew that the pressure inside her would keep building until she flooded it away with the cold, salty, healing caress of the ocean.

It was a hot day, and even the big ceiling fans and the thick stone walls of the old dairy weren't enough to keep away the heat. She closed as usual at five, quickly ate the left-over pasta special she'd served in the tearoom at lunch, rebraided her long hair, grabbed her swimsuit and her towel, and jumped into her car to speed down to the north end of the beach where she could hide among the rocks at the base of the cliff if anyone came.

It was perfect. The beach was deserted and the sky glowed with mauve and orange near the western horizon. There was no wind, but there'd been storms at sea for the past few days and the surf was high, rolling in long, even waves onto the sand. The foam was so white it was almost iridescent.

And the dolphins were there. She tried to surf with them, but they weren't interested tonight. Maybe because her tail hadn't formed yet and they didn't recognize her as a kindred creature. Or maybe because the fishing was good, out where the sea floor shelved down, and eating was more important to them than having fun.

So she surfed alone, and didn't regret the solitude. Didn't use a board, just her body, timing the moment when she launched herself ahead of the breaking wave and let it carry her to the beach in a tumble of cold foam. Her whole body was tingling so much with the buffeting of the waves that it took her a while to recognize the special, deeper sensation that signaled her membrane was starting to form.

And then suddenly she saw him—a strong, athletic-looking man not twenty yards from where she swam. She hadn't noticed his approach at all. He was walking in the shallows and peering out at her, and beyond her, as well, to where the dolphins cruised back and forth, feasting on fish.

Hastily, she waded to shore and ran up the beach to grab her towel, as water streamed from her heavy rope of braided hair and down her torso and legs. When the transformation was imminent, she would wriggle out of her swimsuit and swim naked, but somehow even in this conservatively cut suit, she felt more exposed and more vulnerable this evening than she'd ever felt in the nude.

Why was he watching her?

She was as strongly aware of the stranger's body as she was of her own. She took in the breadth of his shoulders, the length of his thighs and the deep tan of his skin. Beyond these details, he had an aura, a *presence* that she couldn't name. And he was looking at her as if he was seeking something.

She began to rub herself dry immediately. A couple of times in the past, when she hadn't dried the seawater away, her membrane had begun to form as she lay on the sand. From a distance, it had only looked like a rather bizarre and serious case of peeling sunburn, but if anyone had peered too closely...

As this man was. He was studying her with serious intent. Oh, Lord, what had he seen? He was coming over to her, and there was definitely something about him... He was so big and broad and strong, utterly male from top to toe. Look at that long, sure stride! And those eyes! Even in the washed out, dusky light she could see how blue they were, as if filled with the ocean itself.

Filled with the ocean...

She had a strange moment of intuition, and he confirmed it with just one word.

"Thalassa."

Her reaction came at gut level, making a mockery of her recent awareness of him. This wasn't awareness. This was terror.

She scrambled to her feet, screamed and ran toward the headland, fifty yards away. Didn't get far. Not against those long, powerful male legs. He caught up to her within yards and pulled hard on her shoulder to turn her around. His big hand was warm on her cold skin. He let it trail down her arm, and his fingers came within an inch of her breast, leaving an imprint of sensation there as they passed.

"Don't run away, Thalassa," he said. His voice was resonant and deep. "It is you. I knew it. I saw you with the dolphins. And look..."

He dropped his hand to point, and she saw at once what had convinced him. She hadn't rubbed hard enough with her towel. Or else she'd stayed in the water too long.

On her outer thighs there were rough patches of scale, already beginning to flake away. Normally, her tail wasn't like that. When properly formed it was smooth, silvery-green and glistening. But when she left the water at the wrong moment, as she had tonight, the scales were rough and white, and stood out strangely on her skin.

"Who are you?" she said in a voice that refused to work as it normally did. He had her cornered, with the sea at her back, the highest reach of the waves lapping occasionally at her heels, which were still tingling.

She saw a couple strolling along the beach, hand in hand, getting closer every second. She couldn't run past them in a panic. If they tried to help her, how on earth would she explain? And the sea was no refuge. She already sensed that this stranger was far more at home there than she was. So she had to face him, confront him in a way that Cyria's fearful directives had never prepared her for.

He was mer.

He had to be, to have known the name she hadn't heard on anyone's lips since Cyria's death thirteen years ago. Lass registered his clothes—the rough, off-white sailcloth shirt, loosely covering his broad, smooth chest, and the close-fitting sealskin pants that ended, unhemmed, at the knotted swell of his calf muscles. She hadn't seen clothing like this since she was eight.

He was mer, all right.

But who? Her father's messenger? Cyria had always said that Okeana would come for them himself.

The stranger didn't keep her in doubt about his identity for long.

"I am Loucan, son of Galen and now king of the Pacifican people. I have been looking for you for a long time, Thalassa."

"To kill me," she said. Her heart beat even faster. "You're here to kill me, aren't you?"

"No. I'm not your enemy."

"Your father was."

"Things have changed in Pacifica now. We are bringing the two factions together. I have no desire to harm you in any way."

"I don't believe you."

"Then I'll have to convince you. Thalassa, I know this must be a shock for you, after so long. Your father, King Okeana, is dead. You couldn't have known that."

Lass swallowed. "No." But she wasn't surprised at the news. He would have been an old man. In her heart, she had been mourning him for years, certain she would never see him again. "So how did you find me?" she demanded to know, the fear and anger surging through her again.

"It took a long time. But it started when I remembered your beautiful hair...."

Before he could reach her lustrous mass of waves, Lass ran from him, intent on destroying the very thing that led him to her.

Hours later, when he'd left her with his promise—or his threat—to return, and she was lying in her own bed with her now-shorn locks telling herself she was safe, her whole body still refused to stop shaking.

* * *

Lass's hands shook again as she studied the pictures Loucan had spread for her on one of the tearoom tables.

Phoebe's wedding to Kevin Cartwright was the more formal and traditional occasion, but Kai's simple ceremony with rakishly handsome Ben was just as beautiful to Lass's eyes. Both women looked radiantly lovely, with love and happiness sketched in every line of their bodies.

Pictures weren't enough. She wanted to hear their voices, catch up on twenty-five years of lost time, hold them against her and hug them just as she used to when they were tiny.

How would she get through the day?

Looking up, she realized that Loucan wasn't doing what she'd asked him to. Despite what he'd said a few minutes ago about bussing tables and tending bar, and despite his obvious intelligence and strength, she honestly wasn't expecting him to be of much help. He seemed too powerful and too driven to have the necessary practical skills.

Susie had left the chairs stacked upside down on the tabletops after she'd cleaned last night, and Lass had simply asked Loucan to put them back in place. But he'd already done that, and now he was setting the tables, with the deft, experienced movements of someone who'd done this before.

His big hands flicked back and forth, unloading floral centerpieces, place mats, pepper and salt and sugar. The sight was incongruous, but apparently bothered him not at all. Evidently, he didn't set much store by his image when he had a higher goal in view.

Unwillingly, she was intrigued by what this said about the man who now ruled her ancestral home.

As he leaned over the tables, the fabric of his faded jeans tightened over his backside, emphasizing its compact, muscular shape. The sleeves of his T-shirt stretched taut around the hard bulk of his upper arms. Something softened and grew heavy inside her, making her deeply uncomfortable.

She quickly refocused on the photos.

He didn't pause or look up, but he must have seen that she had been watching him, and that she wasn't anymore.

"They've both married good men," he said. "Men who deserve them. Because they're great women, Lass. You'll think so when you meet them again. Both of them are bright and loving and happy."

"Oh, of course they are...."

"Saegar had a tough time, growing up. His guardian, Bali, kept him pretty isolated. He never spent any time on land until he met Beth—her father captured him and was planning to go public. Fortunately, that didn't happen. And when Saegar fell in love with Beth, he made the decision to lose his tail."

"He'll never get it back."

Saegar was one of the cursed among the mer people, able to grow his tail just once. His decision to shed it for the sake of his new love was irreversible. After living as a merman all his life, he must love his new bride very much to have made such a choice.

Lass's chest tightened, as if an unseen hand was squeezing her heart. The idea of taking a step like that frightened her. There was no room for such a dramatic change in her own life. No room for love. Cyria had convinced her of that. Lass was happy here.

She was safe, and she wanted to stay. She had promised Cyria that she wouldn't go back. Pacifica held too many memories.

"Have they decided..." She stopped. Her voice was so scratchy it was barely intelligible. She cleared her throat. "Have they each decided where they'll live now? If they've married land-dwellers, they won't be returning to Pacifica, will they? Even if peace is fully restored there?"

"No. They're all hoping to visit together very soon, but it's not the same."

She expected him to make more of an issue of it, but he didn't. He had his back to her, setting the last of the tables, and she couldn't read him. She knew he hadn't come here just to tell her about her siblings. He wanted something from her. He'd told her that, and instinct told her to dread what it could be.

He obviously didn't want to talk about it yet. Instead, he said in a matter-of-fact way, "I'm finished here. Tell me what you want done in the kitchen, and the gallery."

"The gallery's fine. Everything's set up."

"I liked some of the things I saw, coming through," he said, following her into the adjoining kitchen. "Particularly those semiabstract paintings of the sea."

Yes, those are my favorites, too.

She didn't say it out loud.

"I have a rotating group of local artists and craftspeople who exhibit and sell through the gallery," she explained instead, grabbing on to the subject like a lifeline. "And a stockroom out the back for people to browse through. The tearoom takes more work, but I need both things, to pull in the business. People will stop to browse and stay to eat, or the other way around. I'm not on a main road, so I don't tend to get big tour groups, or anything like that. I'm not making a fortune, but I'm very happy."

And I'm staying.

Her meaning was clear, although she didn't say it.

"Not lonely?"

"With people coming through all day?"

It wasn't an answer, and they both knew it. "People" weren't friends. But she didn't want him to challenge her on any of the choices she'd made in her life. They were necessary, considering who and what she was.

Mer.

Like Loucan himself.

Somehow, though, he was far more at ease inside his own skin than she was. At ease on land, too, from what she'd seen so far. He didn't seem to have built up the same defenses, the same complex web of fear and longing for the mer world, the same deeply ingrained instinct to set herself slightly apart from the land-dwellers among whom she'd lived for so long.

He didn't see his mother die.

"Okay, now salads." Loucan opened her commercial-size refrigerator and began to take out ingredients. "You probably make the quiche fillings and the pastry crusts in advance, right? Just add filling to the base when they're about to hit the oven, a little later on? And are you doing a pasta special?"

"How did you—"

"I read your blackboard menu while I was unstacking the chairs. What about the cakes?"

"Those are delivered. There's a local woman who

makes them for me. But I do the scones. I need to get those in the oven soon.''

''The same as American biscuits, right, only not with gravy?''

''Here we serve them with jam and whipped cream and a pot of tea or coffee, and it's called a Devonshire Tea. They're very popular, all through the day. Even things like sandwiches and pasta people want as late as three or four o'clock.''

''Tricky. Hot dogs or chicken nuggets would be easier.''

''Hot dogs and chicken nuggets would be a disaster. My gallery clientele doesn't have that sort of taste. They want something a little more up market and fancy. I tried a more substantial hot meal for a while. A curry or a casserole. But I found...''

Lass stopped. His face was wooden.

''I'm boring you stupid with this,'' she said.

Lord, what was happening to her, confiding the petty details of her business to him like this? She was rattling on like a runaway train! She, solitary Lass Morgan, who rationed small talk as if words were an endangered species, and never had deeper conversations at all. She was babbling.

Loucan laughed. ''Wait until I tell you about my past life as a bond trader. That'll bore you stupid. This is nice. It reminds me of...well, of some good times I had once, in America, hanging out with someone I liked.''

She went still. ''Don't.''

''Don't what?'' He kept on deftly cutting green pepper and slicing mushrooms with his big hands, while Lass set up the mixer to put together the day's batch of scone dough. Her own hands were clumsy today, and she couldn't seem to get the dough hook to click into its slot.

"Don't try and act as if we're friends," she said. "Don't try to get through to me that way."

She dropped the metal mixing bowl and crossed the kitchen to the CD player. One press of a button brought music into the room—Susie's favorite classic rock radio. Lass didn't care what it was, as long as it was loud and fast and broke the illusion of intimacy.

"Is that what you thought I was doing?" Loucan said. "Trying to get through to you?"

"Yes. Weren't you?"

"I'm not a manipulative man, Thalassa. I don't sneak my way into people's good graces through flattery and insincerity."

His head was held at a proud angle, emphasizing the straight strength of his nose. His brown skin was incredibly smooth, considering he had to be forty years old by now. He was an able man in the prime of life, and Lass felt foolish at having accused him of behaving like a two-faced schoolgirl.

She flushed and said weakly, "Don't you?"

"I go after what I want," he continued. "But I do it openly. I've told you, we'll talk at the end of the day, and then I'm sure things will get rocky and tense again."

"You got that right!"

"I know you don't want this to be happening. For now, if we can enjoy each other's company, is that a sin?"

"I'll...I'll get back to you on that," she told him awkwardly. Lifting the lid of the big flour bin, she would gladly have crawled inside.

A moment later, the driving, upbeat rhythm and

lyrics of a song on the radio threw her back into gear at last. This was familiar. It was what she did every day, and if she didn't get through the routine by ten or close after...

Loucan needed her to tell him what to do from time to time, but apart from that she ignored him. She and Susie and Megan usually chatted a bit. Light stuff about local events and the doings of the women's extended family.

Susie and Megan always did most of the talking, while Lass asked just enough questions to keep the flow going. It was one of the things she liked about the two sisters—the easy flow of their chatter. Since she didn't have to give away much of herself, it kept her feeling safe. Loucan wasn't nearly such a restful presence.

"What time do you usually get your first arrivals?" he asked at around quarter after ten. The clock above the old stone fireplace was ticking loudly, and the scones had just come out of the oven.

"About now."

"I'll wait tables while you take care of things in here. Is that okay?"

"Yes."

If anybody ever showed up. She had been counting on a steady summer crowd today. Like the music, it would add a distance between the two of them that she increasingly needed. It would be ironic if this turned out to be one of their rare days when, for no reason that they could ever predict or discern, almost nobody came.

She hated her awareness of Loucan. Tried to tell herself that it was purely self-defense, but deep down, she knew it was much more.

Loucan was mer.

Lass hadn't seen a merman in twenty-five years, and she'd been just a child then. Over the past fifteen years of her adult life, she had never allowed herself to fall for a land-dwelling man. That one clumsy attempt at a relationship during her college years had quickly convinced her that Cyria was right on this issue. Physically, she and Gordon had never gotten beyond a few unsatisfying kisses.

But Loucan was mer.

That had to be the reason she was feeling like this.

She was so conscious of exactly where he was in the big kitchen. So conscious of her own body—of its lush curves, of its weight and shape and the way it moved, of the sensitivity of her skin.

In the days following one of her guilty trips to the ocean, she was always more sensitized, always yearned for…for *something.* For years this *something* had been quite nameless and out of reach. Painfully, frustratingly so. But suddenly now she understood.

She wanted a man's touch.

She wanted the sensations of lovemaking that she'd only imagined and read about, never experienced. Cyria had told her it must not happen, not with a land-dwelling man. She'd always implied that one day, in the future, when King Okeana came for them and everything was safe, there would then be someone for Lass to give her heart to—someone in Pacifica. Unconsciously, she'd believed that, waited for that.

And Loucan was mer.

Mer, and the son of her father's enemy. It was because of Galen and the escalating violence that her father had secretly sent all four of his children away, each with a different guardian, and each to a different part of the world. It was because of Galen that her mother had died.

The hair on Lass's arms and on the back of her neck stood on end, and her stomach began to churn.

What am I thinking? she wondered. *What kind of a trick is my body playing on me? I can't start wanting him. I still don't know why he's really here. This instinct to trust him could all be coming from…from this physical frustration. Because he's mer, and I want—I want… Oh lord, Cyria was wrong to tell me to live my life like this!*

Chapter Three

"So is it often like that?" Loucan asked.

"No, thank goodness." Lass combed her hand through her hair several times. The gesture was jerky, as if she still expected her fingers to get tangled in the long, living strands that had recently reached to her thighs. As if she couldn't get used to the change.

She looked tired, and Loucan wasn't surprised. It was nearly six-thirty. The kitchen was squeaky clean and the chairs were stacked on the tables. He'd just vacuumed the gallery floor, while Lass was still mopping the tearoom.

They hadn't had a single customer until noon, when three cars had pulled in within two minutes of each other. After that, it hadn't stopped all day. Lass had shuttled back and forth between cash desk, kitchen and gallery, while Loucan had waited tables and washed dishes. He'd also sold two of the seascapes and a big and very ugly vase. He hadn't told her about that yet, actually.

He remedied the oversight, and Lass's opalescent green eyes widened.

"You sold *that?* The big—? The green—? With the knobbly things?"

"Yep. That's the one."

"Good grief, I thought I'd never get rid of that." Her relief broke a little of the simmering tension between them—a tension they'd managed to put on hold since noon.

She leaned on the mop handle. Her hands shook a little and she seemed giddy and light-headed all of a sudden, as if she'd gone beyond exhaustion and was running purely on nerves. Loucan guessed she hadn't been sleeping well since the other night, and felt bad about that.

His fault. And yet he didn't see how he could have softened the blow of his sudden appearance in her life.

"It was left over from an exhibition that didn't do very well," she was saying. "And the artist has left the area, now. How did you manage to—"

"Hypnosis," he told her, straight-faced.

There was a beat of silence, and then she laughed. The sound was a musical gurgle and came from deep inside her. This was the first time he'd seen her do it, and she seemed surprised that it had happened. He got the impression that maybe it didn't happen that often, Lass's pretty laughter. He was sure she spent too much time alone.

Now with her face lit up, her eyes looked greener than ever. The mop handle swayed in her hands, and she swayed with it.

"Lord, I *am* tired!" she said. "I almost believed you."

She laughed again, a lighter, easier sound this time.

"No, seriously," he said, "I just agreed with the customer when she spoke of its lyrical form and the tonal depth of the glaze."

"Yeah? Well, I'm grateful!" She pushed her hair up off her forehead again.

So that she wouldn't have time to regret saying it, he interjected quickly, "Listen, are you done?"

Lass looked vaguely at the floor. "Oh, probably. I've lost track of where I started."

"It looks spotless. You should close up and eat. *We* should eat. Quiche and salad and some limp pasta and stale scones, right?"

"Already packed up in a basket in the kitchen."

"You always live on leftovers from the tearoom?"

"No, sometimes I make some local pigs very happy." She grinned again, and again it did something to him, made him want to get her to laugh and lighten up more often. "But not tonight," she added. "We'll get the leftovers tonight, because I'm too tired to go into town, and the local take-out places don't deliver this far."

She went through her short ritual of locking up, and they walked toward the house, both of them silent until he heard a husky, "Thanks. For today. I would have been swamped. I know you...want something from me, Loucan. You've been honest about that. You didn't have to work your butt off to give yourself a better chance of getting it."

"I know that," he answered. "I wasn't doing that."

"No, I know. I'm going to take it as a reason to at least listen to what you've got to say."

"Not tonight."

"Yes, I want to hear it tonight. Or I won't sleep again, and I need to, because I'm wiped. I've got questions, Loucan."

"Fire away," he invited her.

"How come you're so at home on land?"

Lass wasn't sure why this was the number one question on her list, but after a day spent with Loucan, it definitely was. To her eyes, the other night, he had been so obviously mer. His clothing. His smooth brown skin, nourished by the seawater, which was so much better than any expensive cream or lotion. The way he belonged in the seascape of sky and sand and water. The way he smelled like fresh sea air and salt.

Today, though, he had seemed more at home among the land-dwellers than she was, although she had spent most of her life here. She couldn't believe it when she'd heard him say to the tearoom's first customers, "My name is Luke, and I'll be your waiter today," in his American-flavored accent. Most mer people spoke English with an old-fashioned, almost piratelike lilt, having learned the language from English sailors in the days when Britannia ruled the waves. She'd probably scarcely understand such speech now.

So kings were waiting tables these days? she had thought.

He *acted* like a king, although she doubted he was conscious of the fact. He had every woman he served completely in thrall by the end of the meal. They all promised to come back a second time, and to recommend the place to their friends. The men laughed at his humor. The gallery customers eagerly absorbed his references to Impressionist painting and classical Chinese pottery.

How did he know that stuff?

"I left Pacifica, don't you remember?" he answered her. "About a year before you did."

"No, I...my memories of that whole time are very patchy."

They were overshadowed, blocked out, by what had come after.

"It's not surprising," he said. "You were only eight."

He didn't know what she had seen, and she couldn't find the words to tell him. Lass pushed the memory back, deep down inside her. She led the way into the house, coming through the back door, which opened into the kitchen.

"Do you want to freshen up first?" she invited him.

"No, I'm fine."

"Continue, then. So you left. You must have only been—"

"Fourteen. It wasn't quite running away, but it was close. I told my parents I was going. They weren't happy about it, but I didn't given them a lot of choice. I just went."

Lass took two low-alcohol beers from the fridge. She held one out and he nodded and took it. There were two cracks and two hisses as they opened the cans in unison. Lass put hers down after one mouthful and got out the leftovers to heat in the microwave.

"Why, Loucan?" she said. "Why was leaving so important?"

"Because I couldn't stand what was happening in Pacifica. The factions that were developing, with your parents on one side and mine on the other."

"Where did you stand?"

On Galen's side, of course, she realized abruptly. Why even ask? Why was he here in her kitchen, drinking her beer? Her mother had died at the hands of one of Galen's men.

"I thought both factions were dangerously and completely wrong." The blunt strength of the statement silenced Lass's inner rebellion. "I despised Joran, and I was deeply disappointed in your father for listening to him."

Before she could speak, he continued, "And I thought my own parents were foolish and naive. They wanted to declare Pacifica's existence to the world? They knew nothing *about* the world! And neither did your father, or Joran, or any of the people who argued that whole craziness about mer superiority and using the land-dwellers as we needed them. None of it made sense, because nobody *knew.* The mer people had stayed hidden for so long, apart from a few wild souls who ventured forth to bring back patchy knowledge and exaggerated stories. Both your father's ideas and my own father's beliefs were based on imagination and speculative theories. I wanted to *know.* So I left. A reconnaissance mission, I guess. It lasted over ten years."

"But you were only a child, Loucan!"

"I was strong and big, even among the mer. And I matured quickly. I had to. On land, I passed for twenty when I was sixteen. And during the first two years I didn't spend much time on land. I took it slowly."

"When my mother was killed, shortly after you left—"

"I was riding the Japan current with a pod of whales. I knew nothing about Wailele's death, or the escalation of violence in Pacifica, for another nine years. Does that help, Lass?''

He said it quietly, soberly. She pressed the start button on the microwave and turned to face him. His eyes were fixed on her, his gaze steady and his mouth closed and serious.

''Yes, I guess so,'' she answered. ''If it's true.''

''Why wouldn't it be true? What have I got to gain by lying? We've been alone for hours today. If I wanted to harm you in any way, Lass, haven't I already had ample opportunity?''

''There's more than one kind of harm. You've already harmed me just by coming here.'' Her voice cracked unexpectedly and she swallowed the hard lump in her throat.

''Have I?''

''I was safe. I was happy. I was fine. I didn't know how much I needed...'' She stopped.

How much I needed that ''something'' in my life that I never had a name for until now.

Lord, she could hardly look at him without wondering how it would feel to lie in his arms, to feel his heat and strength around her and inside her.

He was mer, and so was she. It took away all the excuses she'd used to herself over the years for not getting involved with a man, and made her suddenly confront everything that was lacking in her life.

''Why were you dressed in mer clothing the other night?'' Lass posed the question in a desperate attempt to keep her focus.

''Because I hoped it would help you to accept who I was.''

''How did you know you would find me that night?''

"I didn't. I've worn that clothing many times. I've been going up and down the coast for weeks, on and off, in search of you."

"By car?"

"No, I have a boat, which is moored in the harbor at Condy's Bay right now. She's named the *Ondina,* after my mother."

Condy's Bay was only about fifteen minutes' drive from here.

"So you've just been sailing up and down the coast, hoping you might get lucky and spot a red-haired mermaid?"

"I've been talking to different people, trying different stories, and, yes, sometimes just walking the beach watching for dolphins in the water."

She knew what "story" had finally worked. The one he'd fed to Judy at the hair salon. That he was a photographer, looking for a model with long, red-gold hair for a photo shoot involving dolphins. It would help if she was a strong swimmer.

Judy had been only too happy to stay in conversation with such a well-built and good-looking man, and although she hadn't been willing to give Lass's name or address, she'd unintentionally come up with all the details he needed.

The microwave pinged.

"You told me you were an honest man," Lass said. "But you lied to Judy."

"What did you want me to tell her? 'I think one of your clients might be a mermaid I'm looking for. She has long red hair and green eyes, and if you recognize this description could you please give me her address?' I do want, one day, for us to tell the world who we are, but it can't be done like that. It's been pretty hard for Kevin and Ben and Beth to accept the reality of our existence, even with love to smooth the way. It has to be done right."

"How?"

He spread his hands. "I'm working on that. First, and it's starting to happen, we have to end the polarization that has half of Pacifica despising the land-dwellers and half of them idealizing them into paragons of all that is wise and good."

Lass coughed. "Hardly! Once you've experienced—"

"Exactly!" he interrupted. "Once you've experienced life on land. Once you *know*. That land-dwellers are every bit as complex as the mer. That there's good and bad, things that work on land and things that get royally messed up. And you *do* know, in a way that most of the mer still don't, jaded though they are with the fighting. Don't you see what an asset you could be?"

"No!" She dropped a tangle of leftover linguine into a big, shallow bowl, serving tongs included, and paced the kitchen. "I should have known! I should have guessed that's what you wanted. I'm not going back, Loucan!"

Damn!

It was his own fault, Loucan realized. He had allowed his impatience to overpower his judgment. He'd declared himself way too soon, and Lass had made all the necessary leaps of logic. He'd underestimated just how bright and on the ball she was.

True, she hadn't exactly made it easy for him with the direction of her questions. He'd expected her to focus on her siblings. Maybe it was the fault of those wedding photos. She'd lingered over them this morning, absorbing every detail, and asking questions about Saegar as well. She'd obviously satisfied herself that they were all happy. Safe, too, away from Pacifica, and not likely to go back except for cautious visits, including the imminent one they were all impatient for.

"I'm not looking for any kind of decision right away, Lass," he said calmly.

"Well, you're getting one!" Her green eyes blazed and her full lower lip jutted angrily. "My decision is made. I won't go back to Pacifica! There's your pasta. It's getting cold. Let's eat, both of us, because I'm tired. I want to phone Saegar and my sisters, and then I want you to leave."

"This isn't over, Lass."

"Is that a threat? Are you planning to kidnap me?"

Loucan's scalp tightened in frustration. Kidnap her? Yes, what a good idea! Take her to dinner somewhere overlooking the water and talk to her, *listen* to her, until he arrived at a better understanding of why this was so difficult for her. She didn't look like a timid, unadventurous woman. She hadn't been a timid child.

"If I have to," he said. His teeth were clenched.

Lass went white and clutched her hand to her throat. Loucan felt as though his heart had just dropped to the pit of his stomach.

"Hell, I didn't mean it like that!" he told her. "We need more time, that's all."

"We don't!"

"I don't want you to tell me to get lost just yet. There's more that I want from you."

"What *more?*" she asked in a hard voice. "What more, what harder thing, could you possibly ask than for me to go back to the place where my mother was killed, and where my father, you've told me, died in a pitched battle that I knew nothing about?"

"Mine, too, Lass," he reminded her quietly. "My father died, too. Don't forget that."

She ignored him. "You want me to go back to the place where I've believed for twenty-five years that I'd be killed, too, if I returned there without my father's protection."

"Cyria has made you too afraid."

"It wasn't just Cyria."

"Then what was it?"

But she shook her head. "I'm too tired for this tonight."

"Then we'll leave it." He masked his frustration. "I've been too impatient, Lass. I can see that. We'll phone Saegar and your sisters, and then I'll go. But I'll be back tomorrow."

"I'll talk to you again soon, Kai. Yes, I know. Me, too. I can't even put it into words. Yes...oh, yes. Soon. Bye."

Lass set the phone carefully back in its cradle. Her eyes were shining, Loucan saw. She didn't try to hide the tears.

"Whatever..." She cleared her throat and tried again. "Whatever I might feel about the possibility of going back to Pacifica, Loucan. The *dread* I felt when I first found out who you were, and that I've felt since...this makes up for it. I'll never forget that you brought me news of Kai and Phoebe and Saegar."

Her tears spilled, but she was laughing, too. And

her laugh was more free and less rusty than it had been just an hour or two ago.

"I woke them up!" she said. "I woke all three of them up! I forgot that it's the middle of the night in America. I think Phoebe thought that Kevin had been dreaming when he passed the phone across to her and told her it was me."

She laughed harder, more tears came, and she was shaking.

Loucan hadn't intended to take her in his arms. It just happened. With her shoulders jerking and her teeth chattering and tears flooding down her cheeks, what else could he do? He slid his arms around her, cradled her head on his shoulder and soothed her like a little child.

"Shh! Stop this! It's okay. Relax!"

But she didn't. She couldn't. He could feel how stiff and tense her muscles were, and her fingers were digging into his back like crabs digging themselves into the sand. She had her forehead pressed hard into his shoulder, and he just *had* to get her to slow down, let go. Breathe, in fact.

"Criminy! You're at the end of your rope, aren't you?" he whispered. "What can I do? What the heck can I do to get you to let go a little?"

He stroked his fingers lightly over her head, releasing the sweet smell of her shampoo into the air. He did it again, sensing an infinitesimal easing of those knotted muscles. Her neck was warm, the skin there tender and covered in a light down of hair.

It was a long time since a woman had needed this tenderness from him, and a long time since he'd allowed himself to give it. When his hand reached the middle of her back, she turned her head a little, and she wasn't burrowing anymore, nor was she butting his shoulder like a lamb with sore horns. She was nestling.

And still shaking.

"Shh," he whispered again, and pressed his mouth to her temple.

She made a little sound in her throat. At first he thought it was a sob or a protest, but then he realized, no. *No...* This was the thing she needed. Not words. Not even sleep. And certainly not solitude.

This.

He turned her face up to his with a hand cupped around her jaw, and kissed her, pressing his mouth on hers, imprinting her lips with sensation. She made another sound, stronger, and he felt her lips part, sighing a puff of warm breath into his mouth.

Her arms wound around his neck and she swayed, suddenly heavier against him as she let his strong body take her weight. He held her, touched to his depths by her need. Her stomach was pressed against his arousal, and yet she seemed unaware of it.

That wasn't possible, was it? Could she be so very innocent, at the age of thirty-three?

Testing the idea, he dropped his hands to her hips and pulled her gently but firmly closer. He kept on kissing her at the same time, running the tip of his tongue across the sensitive inner skin of her lower lip, softening his mouth on hers so that he could drink her sweet taste.

Her response was immediate and strong. She deepened the kiss and slid her fingers back through his hair, loosening its customary braid until the strand of leather knotted at the end of it slipped off.

Maybe she wasn't the only one who could still betray her innocence, he thought, stunned at the way she was touching him.

He'd made love with more than one woman. He'd been married, and yet he'd never known that his scalp was such an erotically sensitized part of his body. Her fingers were cool and gentle, combing through his hair so that it tickled his neck and shoulders.

Still, she gave no sign that she was aware of the extent of his arousal.

For a few moments longer, she remained lost in their kiss. Her breasts were full and soft against his chest, and he was so tempted to dip his head lower and cover the swollen shapes with the heat of his mouth, through her thin, clingy tank top. Resisting the temptation, he pulled her closer still, and rocked his hips from side to side in a slow arc.

Suddenly, she went still and then stiffened. At last she'd registered the significance of the ridge of pressure bumping her stomach. She tore her mouth from his, looked down for half a second, then up into his face, her eyes wide. Her pupils were huge and black, and her breathing high and shallow.

He didn't know what he had expected. Another kiss, maybe? Even longer, deeper and better than the first. An apology? Instead, she fought her way out of his arms without a word and backed away, one hand closing against her throat as if she could barely breathe.

"Lass—" he began.

"Please leave."

"Not like this."

"Yes. *Yes.* I don't want this. I can't do this. I don't know how."

She turned and fled from the room, and a moment later he heard a door slam at the end of the corridor.

Standing in her room in the dark, Lass watched Loucan's taillights disappear through her open gate and turn onto the road leading to the highway.

"He must think I'm crazy!" she muttered to herself. "Why did I react like that? I'm not crazy, but I'm a fool!"

A fool to have let him see how much his arousal had shocked her. And why had it?

Reasons aplenty.

She'd been shocked at the fact of it, first of all, with its offer of proof that she wasn't the only one feeling like this. For her, it was about an awakening that she knew was long overdue.

She'd been telling herself that it was only because he was mer. She'd told herself that it had nothing to do with any specific chemistry or personality, nothing to do with *him,* Loucan, at all. Instead, she'd begun to convince herself that it had everything to do with how tightly she'd locked her own sensuality away, for the whole of her adult life.

But that couldn't be right, if he felt it, too....

Secondly, she'd been shocked at how long it had taken her to realize what was going on. She'd been so lost—*so lost!*—in their kiss. Even now, in memory, the power of it almost knocked her off her feet like a rogue wave surging against her body. There hadn't been room in her for any conscious thought, until suddenly the melting, swelling sensation deep inside her had struck the vivid contrast of something hard and firm, and she'd understood.

Far too late.

Finally, she'd been shocked at her immediate, incongruous sense of simultaneous longing and exultation and fear. Exultant that it was happening. Longing for it to go further. Absolutely terrified about this level of intimacy.

No one should be this inexperienced at the age of thirty-three.

"What have I done to myself?" she whispered.

It wasn't fair to blame Cyria. It wasn't even right to blame the horror Lass had witnessed as an eight-year-old child.

I made my own choices, she thought to herself. *I took what life gave me, and I chose my response. Not everyone would have ended up like this. A thirty-three-year-old virgin who turns wild with need the moment she lets her guard down a fraction, and then clams up again and runs a mile. I don't know how to handle it. I don't know what to do. What if he thinks he can get what he wants from me this way?*

She dreaded the thought of his return tomorrow.

Chapter Four

"I wondered if I'd find you here," Loucan said.

Lass was with the horses, and it was still early, just seven in the morning. Having heard the distant slam of his car door a few minutes ago, she was prepared for his arrival, but not for his immediate effect on her senses. Her heart began to beat faster as she watched the last few strides of his approach. Her perceptions were heightened and time seemed to slow.

She had plenty of opportunity to see the way his body moved beneath his jeans and blue chambray shirt, plenty of opportunity to observe the dark gold highlights the sun brought out in his hair. It was like the grain in some rich, polished wood, and as usual he had it pulled into a low, tight braid on his neck. She was suddenly sure that somewhere, way back, he'd had a pirate ancestor.

"Some days, at this hour, Loucan, you would have found me in bed!" she retorted.

Her stomach sank. Was that the best thing she

could come up with, having groped several seconds for a reply? Would he think it was a deliberately suggestive line?

She hated reacting this way, but she was on a hair trigger where he was concerned. Her memory of their powerful kiss and her anguished uncertainty about the meaning of her response to him had overshadowed her joy at rediscovering her siblings. Her stomach began a familiar churning.

To her relief, however, Loucan took her words calmly.

"I woke up early," he said. "I always do, on the boat. There's a king tide running this morning. It's spectacular. I swam for over an hour, just as dawn was breaking, watching the waves crashing and foaming onto the headlands and the beaches. There's a little island offshore, just south of Seaview."

"Mullaby Island. Off the end of Possum Point." Lass knew it well.

She'd done the same thing he'd just described many times—naked, since the mer transformation had to involve shedding her swimsuit. Loucan would have been naked in the water, too, his body sleek and powerful, his skin tanned like cinnamon-colored silk.

"I lay out there, in the first rays of the sun," he said. "Felt like it was next door to heaven."

"Today, I'd rather ride," she stated, turning back to the feed trough she was filling. The horses stamped impatient hooves.

Loucan was doing it deliberately, she was sure—using the power of her need for the sea to break down her defenses and remind her of everything they had in common. She was determined it wouldn't work, and could only hope he wasn't aware of her body's growing need for him.

"Got a horse for me?" he asked.

"You ride?"

"Not for a long while. I used to at one time."

"These guys are all pretty frisky," she warned.

There was her own chestnut gelding, Willoughby, and four more horses that she boarded on her land. She fed and watered them and kept an eye out for any problems, in return for a fee. Milo's owner was away at the moment, and Lass was supposed to ride him occasionally. Unfortunately, he was big and young and the friskiest of the lot.

"Try me," Loucan said, and Lass saw the gleam in his eye.

Her heart sank. Did she really think she could scare him off with the threat of a lively horse? His whole personality shouted the fact that he was born to command, and a horse would read and respect the signals as clearly as a human being.

She tried one last time to put him off. "You must be hungry after all that cavorting in the ocean. You don't want to eat?"

"You're bringing a picnic, I notice. I'll wait for that." He gestured at the backpack she wore. It had a flask of hot coffee and two thickly filled bread rolls sticking out of the top. Her brunch.

"I'll be pretty hungry myself soon," she said. "There isn't enough for two."

"You saddle the horses and I'll stretch the picnic with a few more things from the kitchen. Don't fight it, Lass," he added in a lower tone.

The fine hairs on her arm stood on end. "Fight what?"

Had he read her mind? Or just her body language? She was so aware of him that her heart was pounding in her chest and her knees wobbled. He smelled cleanly of soap and seawater, and his square jaw was freshly shaved. Her fingers itched to stroke his face, to discover if his skin was as smooth there as it looked on the rest of him.

She was determined he shouldn't guess how strongly she responded to his presence, but this petty fighting wasn't the way to achieve that.

"Never mind," she added. "Don't answer that. Sure, pack some more food, come for a picnic and a ride. Fruit and cheese and crackers, or whatever you can find. I already have rolls and a flask of coffee and some of yesterday's chocolate mud cake from the tea-room."

"Chocolate mud cake? Yep, you're right," he said. "I'm hungry."

A laugh bubbled out of her. She didn't normally laugh so readily, and it wasn't a particularly funny line, but somehow he did this to her. He made her laugh. He'd made her cry more than once, as well. All her emotions were extra close to the surface since they'd met, and while she could think of other reasons for why this should be so, she knew what the true reason was.

This awakening in her body, longed for and unwanted at the same time. Frightening and seductive. Making her heart and her stomach behave strangely even while her jaw began to ache with the effort of bottling in her feelings.

While he was inside the house gathering the extra picnic things she'd suggested, Lass saddled Willoughby and Milo and turned the other horses loose in their big, grassy field. They cantered away, then slowed to crop the fresh grass, which was still drenched in cool summer dew. The morning sun brought out the rich chestnut and ebony-black on their flanks.

There wasn't a cloud in the sky, and the horses seemed to appreciate the fact as much as humans did. Willoughby made a snickering sound, and Milo flicked his black tail and pricked his ears forward.

Lass was thankful for the time alone, and for the horses. She was familiar with them. They gave her strength, as they always had, reminding her that she wasn't just a prisoner of her heritage and her past. There was more to her than that—a whole lot more to her than her unusual innocence and her haunted relationship with the sea.

When Loucan emerged from the house, Lass was already mounted and leading Milo alongside Willoughby in the direction of the kitchen door.

"All set," he said. He was wearing the second backpack she kept on a hook behind the door, and he carried a battered object in his hand. He held it up. "Is the hat okay?"

"To borrow it? Sure, why not?"

He'd found her old Akubra—the traditional Australian stockman's hat, equivalent to a Texan's Stetson and made of felt. Lass almost always wore it outdoors. Last year, she'd bought herself a new one in dark gray, but secretly she still preferred this old brown one with its creases and its worn places. An Akubra wasn't a real hat until it had traveled a few hundred miles on horseback or a few thousand in a farmer's pickup truck.

On Loucan it looked like a classic, creases and holes included, and she couldn't help telling him so.

"Thank you, ma'am."

He drawled the words like an American cowboy as he tipped it into his hand, then slapped it low onto his head once more, climbed through the post-and-rail fence and swung himself into Milo's saddle. The animal shifted his feet a couple of times, then settled as if he recognized the feel of experienced hands on the reins.

"Where are we headed?" Loucan asked.

"Across the paddock." She used the Australian word for field. "Through the gate and onto one of the forestry trails. It leads to a creek. I like to stop there and...well, listen to the birds, and to the water. It's nothing like the sea," she added, and knew that she sounded far too defensive. "The sea sighs and roars. The creek gurgles over the rocks. It's less dramatic, but more musical. We might hear kookaburras laughing, too. They're only birds, but they sound exactly as if they're all enjoying a great joke."

"Sounds good," he said. "I love the smell of the air here."

"It's the eucalyptus. The leaves release some of their oil into the air. I've heard that's what makes the skies so blue here, too. The oil in the atmosphere intensifies the color."

"It's true I've never seen skies quite as blue as this."

They rode in silence until after they'd passed through the gate. Lass dismounted and opened it, and Loucan led Willoughby through, managing with ease what could sometimes be an awkward maneuver.

"You must have ridden a lot, at one time." It wasn't quite an accusation on her part, but almost.

"When I was married," he answered. "My wife was an Arizona rancher's daughter."

"You're married? Or, no, you *were*. Once."

"We were divorced a long time ago," he said. "It's been, what, around seventeen years since I sat a horse. For a couple of years, I rode nearly every day. I got to like it. It was one of the few things that made up for how much I missed the sea."

"Tell me what else you want from me, Loucan," Lass begged him suddenly. "It's too hard like this. Just waiting for you to say it. Hearing the way you keep bringing the sea into our conversation. You want me to go back to Pacifica and I've said that I—" *Can't,* she almost said "—won't. What else could be important enough to keep you away from the place, when you've told me that the situation there still isn't stable?"

He looked across at her for a moment, the wide brim of the hat shadowing his brilliant eyes, then said, "Okay. You're right. It's time to say it. And it's quite simple. I want your quarter of the key. I thought you might have guessed."

"Key? What key?"

"I've noticed you're not wearing it, but you were when you left Pacifica, and you must have it somewhere. Okeana had it strung onto a necklace. Cyria would never have let you lose it."

She frowned at him. "I've never had a key from Pacifica. Or a necklace."

"Okeana wanted you to wear it always," Loucan said, persisting in spite of her denials.

His thought processes seemed sluggish to him this morning. Maybe it was that eucalyptus tang in the air.

Or maybe not.

He hadn't been sleeping well since he'd found Lass. Between his impatience to get back to Pacifica and his realization that he had to take things slowly with Lass, his nerves were stretched tightly.

"But I don't have it," Lass said. "I know nothing about a Pacifican key."

Her blank face disconcerted him. Phoebe, Kai and Saegar had each been wearing their portion of the key like a talisman, even though the twins hadn't had any inkling about the significance of the unusual piece of jewelry. Lass, on the other hand, the only one of Okeana's children old enough to remember leaving Pacifica, claimed not to know anything about it.

Unless her apparent innocence was a pretense... Loucan wondered. Mistrust could cut both ways. So far he'd spent all his energy trying to overcome her doubts and fears. He'd been so busy trying to gain her trust, he hadn't questioned whether he had any reason not to trust her in return. A flash of suspicion darted into his mind. Could she possibly be in touch with Joran?

There were so many contradictions to what he'd seen in her so far. Thirty-three years old, and so innocent she didn't recognize when a man was aroused? Able to surf joyously among a school of dolphins, yet so guilty about her need for the sea that she spent half her life fighting to pretend to herself that it didn't exist? Maybe all her fear and doubt was a performance, designed to throw him off.

She *had* to know about the key...didn't she?

Then he remembered another, long-ago line of Cyria's. "For your own good, my little princess." Another possibility occurred to him.

"Cyria could have kept it for you," he said aloud. "Kept it secret, hidden among her things. She might have taken the necklace from you without telling you of its significance, and in time you forgot that it even existed. But one of you must have had it. Must still have it."

"No, Loucan." Lass shook her head, sounding very sure of her ground.

He kept on pushing. "It's in the shape of a quarter circle, about two inches across. She died nearly thirteen years ago, isn't that right?"

"Yes. When I was twenty."

"And she left you all her possessions, in her will?"

"Yes. I was astonished," Lass said.

She frowned and shook her head, and Loucan watched the way memory unfolded on her face. A tinge of pink came into her cheeks, her green eyes seemed to darken, her lips parted a little and the tip of her tongue touched her upper lip for a moment. For a woman who had spent so much time and effort on hiding who she really was, her emotions showed very clearly. Or was that something new, something to do with him?

Milo quickened his pace and Loucan held him back so that he could still see Lass's face as she talked. The sun caught the side of her jaw, emphasizing its strong yet graceful line. The air was filled with the scent of the Australian bushland and the percussive sounds of the horses. It was one of those days when it was good just to be alive. Briefly, Loucan wished he could simply enjoy the feeling, and forget the goals that drove him so hard.

"We'd always lived so frugally," Lass was saying. "I thought we could barely make ends meet. Cyria worked cleaning houses. Wouldn't consider retirement, even when it began to get too much for her. She was so stubborn, and always thought she knew best."

"I remember that," Loucan said. "I wondered if that trait might intensify, over the years."

"She was determined I should get a business degree so I could look after myself. I assumed that was because we had nothing to fall back on. It always seemed strange to me that my father would have sent us away with nothing to help us."

"But Lass, he didn't."

"No, I realized that after her death. Cyria herself never mentioned the subject, and any questions I asked, she deflected. She gave me a watch for my sixteenth birthday, the kind that's set in a solid gold bangle. It was the only expensive gift she ever gave me, and I thought she must have saved for months to buy it. I was so touched by that. Then when she died and I found she'd left me thousands of dollars worth of gold and pearls—enough to buy the old dairy and the farmhouse and several acres of land, restore the whole place and set myself up in business—I was just *astonished!*"

"It was in character," Loucan said. "She retained her mistrust of land-dwellers and her desire to protect you until the very end."

"Yes, she did." Lass smiled. "She loved me. I never doubted that. It didn't take the treasure she'd left me to prove it."

"But there was no quarter circle? It's made of a silvery metal, very distinctive, with some Pacifican symbols etched into it. Nothing like that among the gold and jewels she left you when she died? There *must* have been!"

"No, Loucan. I'm sorry. There wasn't."

Hearing it in such simple words, he had to believe her, and she carried even more conviction when she continued, "Believe me, if I knew anything about it, I'd be only too glad to hand it over."

"Because it would get me out of your life?"

"Yes." She tilted her head to look at him. Their horses clopped along the hard, dry dirt road, sending little swirls of warm summer dust into the scented air. "*Would* it get you out of my life, Loucan?"

Her voice was a little lower and a little huskier than usual, and the dark felt hat sat low on her forehead, darkening her eyes. They were sea-toned, instead of iridescent green opal. In the bright light, the hair that curled just below the hat's brim looked like flame.

Loucan shook his head slowly.

"No. It wouldn't get me out of your life," he said. "You know there's no going back, Lass."

"There is, if I choose! Once you leave—"

"No," he repeated. "You want to stay in contact with Saegar and your sisters. For better or for worse, Pacifica is a part of your life again. I won't pretend that it's pure, unadulterated good news. Joran is still on the loose, playing his old games."

"I'm starting to remember Joran...."

"He's gotten even more dangerous now that he no longer has your father's backing. He traced Phoebe through my search for her, and her life was in danger at one stage. We know he's after the four sections of the key."

"Why is it so important? What is it a key *to,* Loucan?"

"To Pacifica's hidden archive of scientific knowledge. Your father locked it away when the unrest began. He thought it would only add to the danger. Joran believes—and maybe he's right—that if he can control and make use of that knowledge, he can hold power. I can't let that happen. He's driven purely by ego, and he would lead our entire people to destruction."

"Where are the other quarters of the key? You said my siblings had them? Surely that puts them in danger!"

"They've given them to me, and I have them hidden at sea for safekeeping. No one but me now knows where they are. I won't risk Joran getting his hands on them."

"If anything happened to you, they might never be found."

"Better that than to risk them getting into the wrong hands. I want you to think, Lass, and I want you to go through Cyria's things again. Could she have hidden your part of the key somewhere? Buried it or put it in a bank vault? Did she ever say something to you that in hindsight might have been a cryptic clue?"

"Loucan, I—"

"I'm not expecting you to come up with a miracle on the spot."

"That's good," she drawled, "because I'm running a little low on miracles today."

"In fact, let's forget the whole thing for now. Let your subconscious work on it, and maybe it will throw something into the light. Are we getting close to your musical creek?"

"Yes, the trail is to the right, just over this rise."

She urged her horse on a little faster, and Loucan dropped behind, content to watch her rear view and leave further talking for later. When they reached the creek, she dismounted at once, led Willoughby down to drink, then turned him loose to graze.

"Milo, too?" Loucan asked.

She nodded. "There are fences running parallel to this trail on both sides. You can see them through the trees. Even if the horses do wander off, they can't go far. I've got some treats in my backpack to make them come running."

"Picnic time, then. Did you bring a blanket to sit on?"

"Uh, yes. Yes, I did." She looked a little self-conscious. Goose bumps rose on her arms as if she was cold in her short-sleeved, pale blue T-shirt, and when she'd spread the blanket on a patch of dapple-shaded grass, he understood why.

It wasn't meant for two...unless those two happened to be lovers.

Lass clearly didn't know what to do about the problem. A lot of the women he'd known would have used the opportunity to flirt, but even if she knew how—and he doubted she did—she obviously wasn't planning on flirting with him.

He thought back to yesterday's kiss, and it disturbed him. In theory, those long, intense moments in each other's arms should have played right in the direction he wanted. From the time when he first began his search for Okeana's children, he'd hoped for a strategic marriage with one of the three Pacifican princesses. Kissing Lass was the closest he'd gotten to realizing that goal.

And yet, although it didn't make sense, he couldn't help wondering if the unplanned kiss had been a huge mistake.

Without it, he might not have suspected just how innocent she was. Now that he knew, her innocence wasn't something he could ignore. Coupled with the passionate sensuality of her response, it added up to a woman he could very easily hurt. An emotionally volatile woman who might not be able to contemplate the cool-headed political alliance he was looking for.

With the restless, questing life he'd led in his late teens and early twenties, Loucan had hurt women before. His ex-wife, Tara, had suffered, through his cowardly inaction, the kind of hurt that no woman every truly forgot. His guilt over that had been terrible. He'd questioned everything he believed, and everything about the man he'd become. In the end it was what had impelled him back to Pacifica.

There, he had sworn off the whole idea of love. He'd loved Tara once, but not enough to act in a way that might have saved their marriage. He didn't want the same kind of power over a woman's happiness a second time. He didn't trust his capacity to give that much.

The last thing he wanted, therefore, was that Lass should fall in love with him, and he had no intention whatsoever of falling in love with her. He still wanted to marry her, though. He just didn't know if he dared.

Hands off, he decided silently to himself. *That's the only way this can work. I can't kiss her again.*

"Did you want me to...? I—I mean, there's room," Lass stammered, drawing his focus away from strategic questions. Her cheeks had gone pink once more. She shifted her firm, shapely backside six inches toward the edge of the plaid picnic blanket. The movement rocked her hips gracefully. "Please sit down!"

Loucan realized that he had been standing there for an embarrassing interval, staring down at the blanket without even seeing it. She must have thought he was waiting for an invitation to sit beside her.

He did so, and at once arrived back at square one.

This blanket wasn't big enough for two.

Maybe it was the calculated decision not to—*definitely* not to—kiss her again, but he was suddenly very aware of just how easy a kiss would be. She had her legs curled to one side and her weight resting on the other hand. The only way he could sit comfortably was in a mirror image of the same pose. It brought his shoulder within a few inches of hers.

He could smell her, too. He could tell that she'd washed her hair this morning, that she was wearing sunscreen and that her cotton T-shirt had been line-dried in the fresh air. It was a very close-fitting top. The short sleeves just capped her shoulders, and below them her fair, tender skin stretched over smooth arm muscles.

If he moved his hand three inches to touch her fingers… If he leaned a little closer and she turned her head his way… Yes. He would reach her mouth and taste those warm, passionate lips again.

"Can I start with the mud cake?" he asked, in an iron-willed attempt to think of something besides her full, gorgeous mouth.

She laughed, eased the weight off her hand and sat up straighter. "If you were a child, I'd have to say no, wouldn't I? You're not supposed to start with dessert. But, yes, let's. I'm in the mood for chocolate, too."

She was still smiling, and still pink-cheeked, as she used a pocket knife to cut the thick wedge of cake she'd brought. When she handed half to him, he carefully took it without letting their fingers touch, but this turned into a wasted effort. He'd accidentally smeared some of the thick, gooey frosting onto her thumb, and his gaze was trapped by the sight of her mouth and tongue as she licked it off.

The action was delicate, yet astonishingly sensual. The tip of her tongue darted forward to scoop the smear of frosting, then her lips closed over the spot and she sucked it clean. Finally she looked at it and gave it one last, expert lick, like a cat lapping at a saucer of milk.

If she knew I was watching her like this...

Maybe she'd sensed it. Taking a slow, careful mouthful of cake, she turned toward him and smiled. "Better to let it melt in your mouth than in your hand."

Loucan shifted his focus just in time. "I guess it is," he said, and took a bite, barely tasting it.

He didn't understand it. He'd been attracted to mer women and land women before. What was different about Lass? The fact that she was such an intriguing mixture of both?

Or was it the lure of forbidden fruit?

He had just told himself categorically that he must not kiss her again, which meant, in the perversity of the male psyche, that now he wanted to kiss her all the more. He wanted her mouth and tongue to do to his skin—every inch of his skin—exactly what they'd just done to that smear of chocolate frosting. With exactly the same skill, and exactly the same attention to detail.

He cleared his throat behind his fist. "Are Susie and Megan coming to work today?"

"Yes, thank goodness," Lass said. "That's the only reason I had time for a ride this morning."

"And would you also have time to show me Cyria's things when we get back?"

"What makes you think I'm prepared to do that?"

Lass lifted her chin and narrowed her eyes deliberately, although she was sure her attempts to act cool this morning weren't fooling him. He was watching her. She knew he was. He had to be looking for signs of how vulnerable she was. He would remember the way she'd kissed him. That kind of response didn't go away overnight, did it?

Even sitting as straight as a Victorian schoolmarm in a whalebone corset, she couldn't get far enough away from him on this blanket. He knew what he did to her. The only thing she could do was to make it clear that her attraction to him didn't make her vulnerable, after all. She wasn't going to give him everything he asked for.

She expected him to argue, but he didn't. "Are you planning to go through them yourself?" he asked instead.

Maybe he could read her mind. The mer weren't psychic, but so far he'd been pretty good at reading her body language, and her emotional needs. On this occasion, there was no point in lying to him.

"Yes, when I get a chance," she answered him. "Carefully. When I'm not tired. Or distracted. Otherwise there's no point in doing it at all. If there was any obvious information about the whereabouts of the key, I'd have found it before this. If Cyria did leave me a message, or a clue of some kind, it's pretty well hidden."

"Which means I'd have more chance of finding it than you would, since I'm far more familiar with mer culture, and with the symbols she might use."

"I'm not showing you her things, Loucan." Lass didn't need any more opportunities for him to watch her emotional barriers breaking down.

"It's your decision," he answered.

"Yes. Remember that!"

She glared at him again, feeling like a mother bird trying to protect its nest from a marauding cat. She could chirp and flutter all she wanted, but in the long run she doubted that her behavior would change the outcome. He would prowl, undeflected, toward his goal.

They ate the salad rolls, the fruit, cheese and crackers, washing the meal down with strong coffee followed by fresh water from the stream.

"Tell me why you love this place so much," he said, and she couldn't see any danger or intent behind the question, so she told him.

"Not hard to understand, is it? The beauty. The peace. The fact that it's unspoiled enough that we can drink the water from the creek and not get sick."

"And why the gallery, and the tearoom?"

"I like selling beautiful things that people will treasure."

"Like the green vase?"

She had to laugh. "Well, the woman who bought it obviously thought it was beautiful and worth treasuring."

"True."

"And I like serving meals that give people pleasure."

"Yet you don't trust people—land people—very much, do you?"

Her scalp tightened, and so did her mouth. "I should have known you weren't just making casual conversation, Loucan. What point are you trying to prove this time? That I'm not truly at home here, so I should go back with you to Pacifica?"

"I wasn't trying to prove a point. I was just making an observation."

"A very pointed observation. Okay, yes, I don't trust people. Can you blame me? Should I have a heart-to-heart talk with Susie over the scone dough one day? She's started throwing out hints about how satisfying marriage can be, and how if you want to meet a good man you have to go out and find one, not just sit back and wait for it to happen. Should I tell her, 'Well, actually, yes, I'd love to meet a man, only, you see, I grow gills and a tail when I stay in the water too long, and I'm not sure if he'd be able to deal with that.'"

"Susie and Megan are the kind of people you should tell," he insisted. "People you trust."

"But I *don't* trust them! Not enough to be sure they'd react the right way. I've never met anyone I trust that much."

"Because Cyria taught you not to."

"That's part of it. What about you, Loucan?" she asked desperately. "You were married to a land woman, once. Did you tell her that you were mer?"

She hadn't expected it to be a match-winning question, but she could see at once that it was. She'd gotten through to him. She'd distracted him. Was it possible that she'd actually *hurt* him?

His silence was so significant that even the noisy bushland seemed to go still. A group of kookaburras in a distant tree stopped their laughing, and Willoughby lifted his head from the grass to listen, as if suspicious of the change in atmosphere.

"No, I didn't tell her," he finally said. "But still, after more than sixteen years, I wish from the bottom of my heart that I had."

The grief and anger in his face shocked Lass. She wanted to probe more deeply, but something told her not to. Painfully aware of her own vulnerability as she was, the last thing she'd expected to find at the core of a man like Loucan was a well of regret and pain this powerful.

She began to understand that at some level, despite his outward strength and success, the regret made him as vulnerable as she was.

Chapter Five

"Oh, Cyria, I think you kept everything!" Lass whispered aloud.

She brushed tears from her eyes with the heel of her hand, then fumbled in her pocket for a tissue to do the job properly. She had been through her guardian's things before, but not this thoroughly. This time, Lass opened every box, every packet and every envelope, and came across hoarded memories of her own childhood that threatened to overwhelm her.

Every merit certificate from gymnastics or piano, every school report card, every clumsy handmade craft item, had all been carefully preserved, labeled and put away. There was her costume from the school play when she was ten years old, wrapped in blue tissue paper. And a photograph of her shaking the principal's hand and collecting an award.

But no matter how hard she looked, there was nothing about a Pacifican key. No cryptic message. No small, insignificant box that had escaped Lass's attention in the past. Completely satisfied of this fact, she packed the boxes away again. She would break the bad news to Loucan as soon as she saw him again.

"Whenever *that* happens to be!" she muttered aloud to the contents of her attic storeroom.

The day before yesterday, after their ride, she'd gritted her teeth in preparation for dealing with him for the rest of the day, but he hadn't stayed.

"I'm leaving," was all he had said. "I'll be back."

But he hadn't said when.

It was getting to her, fraying her already tightly wound nerves. Where had he gone? All the way back to Pacifica? To America, to see her siblings? Or could he be in trouble—even in danger?

Lass came down the narrow stairs from the attic and closed the door. The low space was directly beneath the roof and stifling hot in the late afternoon. She was damp all over, and the airless atmosphere had made her feel queasy.

The queasiness was nothing to do with any concern for Loucan's safety, she told herself. The life he'd led surely proved that he could look after himself.

But she could remember Joran more clearly now. Old memories had been disturbed like roosting bats, and had swarmed back into the light of her conscious mind. Joran must only have been around eight or nine years older than Loucan himself. He was a cocky, intense and highly intelligent young merman who'd somehow captured her father's interest with his wild ideas.

Yes, she remembered being jealous of him as a child. Her father was always locked in endless conversations with him. He'd never had time, anymore, to tell her the wonderful stories she loved. If she tried to get King Okeana's attention, or to make him laugh, Joran always told her with an insincere smile, "Run along, sweet little princess. Your daddy has more important things to do right now."

Lass shivered suddenly, despite the heat. No, she'd never liked him.

Surely, though, he was no match for Loucan's strength and drive and knowledge!

The possibility of a bloody encounter between the two men, in Pacifica itself or somewhere at sea, haunted her too vividly, and she felt another wave of nausea as she went out into the hot sunshine. Loucan had made her care so much in such a short time. If something had happened to him and he just never showed up... If she had to go on with her old life, never knowing what had become of him, and exiled from Pacifica...

Exiled! What a word to use! She'd never felt that way before. Even the possibility of seeing her siblings again and starting to build a relationship with them couldn't fully make up for the devastating effect Loucan had had on her, and on the way she felt about her life.

He was right in what he had said to her two days ago.

There was no going back.

For no good reason, she went across to the tearoom and opened it up. Today was Tuesday, the one day in the week when the place was closed. Susie and Megan had stayed late last night, and they were very thorough. There was nothing that needed to be done before tomorrow, nothing with which to occupy her restless hands.

When Lass came out again, she saw the ocean sparkling blue and bright in the distance, and it called to her spirit with painful intensity. She groaned aloud. On a hot day like this, in the middle of summer break, all the beaches would be crowded. The water would be warm and her tail membrane would form and thicken quickly. After dark it might be safe, but not yet.

Still, she couldn't take her eyes away…until she saw a dark blue car coming up the road. Her heart lurched. Loucan? There were plenty of cars around like the one he had rented.

If he guessed how lost and empty and restless she had felt since he left, he would use the fact somehow, she was sure of it. All the same, she found she had to keep watching the car, almost holding her breath. It disappeared into a dip, then reemerged, climbing the hill. If it didn't slow down soon, that would mean it wasn't coming here….

But it did slow, at the last moment. It was turning. In another second she recognized Loucan at the wheel.

She began to hurry toward the house, pretending she hadn't seen him, then flinched when he called her name a few moments later.

"Thalassa, wait!"

Turning slowly, she watched and waited, wanting to pour out half a dozen questions, and practically biting her tongue in order to keep them back.

What happened? Did you plan to stay away for so long? Where have you been?

She knew he had been somewhere, because she'd gone down to the harbor at Condy's Bay to look for the boat he'd told her about. The *Ondina*, named after his mother. It wasn't there. He must have taken it out to sea, and now he'd returned.

"Here!" Reaching her, he didn't give her time for questions, just dropped something cold and slightly ticklish into her hand.

"Loucan...?"

"It's Phoebe's key," he said. His blue eyes held no light of awareness or pleasure at seeing her again. Instead, they seemed clouded and dark with his preoccupation. "I brought it from where I'd hidden it so you could actually see it and feel it in your hand. If you've even seen a picture of something like this. If Cyria ever doodled these markings somewhere, or—"

"I've told you," Lass said in a cold tone. "I've never seen it."

She didn't look at the key, nor at the length of slippery metal chain it was strung on. Closing her fingers tightly around it, she felt it quickly grow warm with the heat of her anger.

"Do you think I'm stupid?" Her voice rose. "Do you think Cyria was? I've just been through her things again, because you asked me to, this time practically with a magnifying glass. It took hours. And there's nothing! How likely is it that she'd manufacture a clue so cryptic and well-hidden that I might throw it out with the paper recycling and never realize its existence? How clever would that be? Here I've been, worried that somehow Joran—"

"Joran?" Loucan exclaimed. "You've heard from him?"

"*No!* You're completely single-minded about this, aren't you?" He still hadn't looked at her properly. Not the way she wanted him to, heaven help her, with a warm light of pleasure and desire in his eyes. "It hasn't occurred to you that I might have been concerned about your safety, after everything you've told me. That I might have been on tenterhooks the entire time because you never said where you were going, *why* you were going or when you'd be back. *Shoot!*"

Swearing didn't help.

She covered her face with her hands, took several deep breaths in an effort to win back some control. She'd never let her emotions flood out like this, not in all the twenty-five years she'd lived on land. Willing her shoulders to relax and her awareness of him to subside to a manageable level, she looked up to find him watching her closely at last. He hadn't moved.

"I don't want you to care about me, Lass," he said. The words were as hard and blunt as the old ax blade she used to split kindling wood in winter. "Not in any personal sense. That's not what I'm looking for."

"Good, because I *don't* care," she replied, wanting it to be true. Wanting to *make* it true. Her attraction to him was meaningless. It was purely the product of the solitary, mistrustful life she'd led. She *knew* that! "I just needed to know what was going on."

"And I'm sorry you've lost sleep over it."

"Did I say I'd lost sleep?"

"You look as if you have. There are circles under your eyes." Stepping closer, he traced his thumb lightly over the sensitive skin there. She gave a little shiver of need, and tried to hide the movement by wrapping her bare arms across her body.

"And *I've* lost sleep," he added. "I wish all of this wasn't so hard for you, Lass. Please believe that."

She tucked in one corner of her mouth and drawled, "I'll try."

"Are you busy tonight?"

"Uh...no."

She was never busy at night.

There again, maybe Cyria had been wrong. If Lass had close friends to spend time with, maybe the sea and the dolphins wouldn't call to her so often. If she didn't go for all those guilty, lonely swims, she wouldn't feel so set apart. She might have built a real life for herself here, with the husband and kids that Susie kept naively hinting about.

And if Lass had a life of her own, she wouldn't be half so vulnerable to Loucan.

No, but Cyria wanted this, she realized.

Cyria had never wanted Lass to put her roots in too deep, in case the time came for them to go back. She wanted Lass always to be open to Pacifica's call.

"Let's go to dinner, somewhere by the water," Loucan said. "Let's forget the key for tonight." He took it from her—she still had it dangling in her hand—and she let it go without protest, ignoring the touch of his fingers. "I'll take you out in the boat somewhere safe, and we can swim. You've been lonely, Lass, away from your own kind, and taught to distrust the people around you. Whatever happens in the future, let me help you not to be lonely for a while."

With the need that had been building inside her for so long, Lass couldn't resist his appeal. She didn't care that he knew just how vulnerable she was, didn't care about his hidden and not-so-hidden motivations. Here was someone with whom, in a vital way, she didn't have to pretend, the way she pretended with everyone else.

She hadn't known how deeply she craved this openness until she found it.

"I—I'd like that," she said. "Just for tonight."

"Dress up a little," he suggested. "We'll go somewhere nice. Celebrate the fact that you have siblings again. Have you spoken to Saegar and the twins since the other night?"

"Yes, Phoebe called me yesterday. She and the others are planning their visit to Pacifica, and wanted to know if they could meet up with me at the same time. I said… Well, that it was hard to get away from this place. They may make a detour here. I spoke to Saegar, too. He's still busy getting adjusted to his new life, and isn't sure yet if he'll go with Phoebe and Kai. I think he may stick pretty close to home and Beth."

"Your eyes light up when you talk about them, Lass. If ever you think you have reason not to trust me, I hope you'll remember that I'm the one who brought them back into your life, and I'm the one they trusted with their portions of the key."

"You don't need to remind me of that, Loucan," she told him with a flash of spirit that felt good. "If I didn't trust you in that sense, you wouldn't still be here on my property, and I wouldn't be having dinner with you tonight."

Without waiting for his reply, she went inside to change, thinking, *When it comes to the question of trust, the person I trust least, right now, is myself.*

They drove to a seafood restaurant overlooking the ocean just north of Condy's Bay. It was attached to a solitary hotel on a high headland with magnificent sweeps of white beach to the north and south. The coastal towns south of Sydney were not noted for the formality of their dress code, and Loucan blended in perfectly in his casual dark gray pants and paler shirt.

Or rather, the clothing blended in. The man never could. He was taller and broader than most of the other male diners, and when women's eyes discreetly followed the two of them across the room, Lass noticed at once, and didn't think it was her own little black dress that held their interest, nor even Cyria's heavy and distinctive gold bangle watch on her wrist.

Their meal was wonderful, and a treat for someone who spent so much of her time on the opposite side of a kitchen door. Wanting to keep the conversation to safe topics, she reminded Loucan of his threat to bore her with stories about bond trading in New York.

But he'd been kidding her, of course. His stories weren't boring at all.

"Cyria used to try and get me interested in money," Lass told him. "She wanted me to get an accounting degree, while I leaned toward something creative. We compromised on business management. But the way you tell it, there's a lot more drama in dollars and cents than there is in scones and cream."

"A lot more stress, too," he answered. "Riding with you the other day, and tasting the water from the stream, I started to understand. There's more to what you have than just a place to hide."

She nodded, and said with spirit, "Of course there is. But you're right. I—I have been hiding. For too long."

She played a little self-consciously with Cyria's gold bangle. Catching sight of the time indicated by the long, ornate gold hands, she was surprised to find that it was still not even eight o'clock. They'd arrived here quite early. There was still plenty of evening ahead.

"Do you want coffee or dessert?" Loucan asked.

Their waiter was hovering. Outside, the sun was beginning to set, changing the colors of the water and turning the sand into silver and gold. Even in this magnificent setting, Lass began to feel confined and eager for some fresh air.

Either Loucan sensed this, or he felt it, too. As she framed her reply, he added, "It suits me if you don't. We could go for a walk along the beach here, before we drive back to the boat."

She nodded. "And maybe later on, as soon as it's fully dark, we can..." Her voice went husky and she cleared her throat. "We can go for that swim."

"Yes, I'd like to swim with you tonight, Thalassa."

She flushed, hearing a connotation to the words that she was sure he didn't intend. It wasn't his fault that the sea and her own sensuality were so closely linked in her mind. He didn't know that after she'd immersed her body in seawater, she always longed more strongly for the unknown mystery of a man's intimate touch.

Oh, Lord, and she didn't *want* him to know, either!

She took care not to touch him as they left the restaurant.

Barefoot a few minutes later, with their shoes left in the car, they scrambled down the steep cliff path to the beach and walked north toward the next headland. The sibilant sigh of the waves on the sand kept their silence from feeling awkward. When the ocean was speaking, there was little need for other conversation.

The beach was dotted with people tonight. Surfers and fishermen, children playing ball, couples walking hand in hand. It was too crowded to swim yet. If anyone saw them disappear out to sea, and raised an alarm, thinking they were in danger, the consequences could be frightening.

Lass had been "saved" once in the past by an overeager lifeguard, just before her tail began to form. She'd been petrified of discovery. Cyria would have yelled about it for weeks, had she known, and Lass herself had no desire to repeat the experience.

And yet she longed for the sea.

"Do you want to turn back?" Loucan asked when they reached the end of the beach.

"No, how about we go across the picnic area to the tidal inlet," she suggested. "The tide has just started going out, which means the current at the mouth of it will be strong. Almost no one swims across the inlet then, and there's no way through to the next beach by road. We won't need swimsuits, and we won't need to wait. That beach will be..." She stopped, realizing that she was speaking too fast and much too eagerly.

"Empty." He finished for her, smiling. "Don't be ashamed of your impatience. It reminds me of when you were a child, always so brave and eager. I'm glad you haven't lost that spirit, Lass."

"Mmm." She turned away, not wanting him to see her face.

There were families cooking barbecue at the public gas grills in the park, and children splashing in the inlet. The sun had just set behind the mountains to the west, and the light was draining out of the sky, turning into a dozen different pastel shades as it went.

"Watch out for broken oyster shells on the rocks and mangrove trunks," Lass warned Loucan. "They're sharp. Stick to the sand, or you can get cut."

"Should those kids be playing on the rocks, then?"

She gazed in the direction he was pointing, and saw several children messing around on the rocks. They ranged in age from preteen down to toddler, and looked like siblings. She couldn't see their parents.

"Those rocks are probably free from oyster shells. They're just above the high tide line. But the current starts to get strong around this point," she said. "If I was a parent—"

Loucan didn't wait for the end of her sentence. With an exclamation under his breath, he took off ahead of her through the shallow water, and she saw that the youngest child had just lost his balance and slipped off the rock he was standing on. Lass lost sight of him beneath the water for several seconds, then he sat up in water that reached to his chest, spluttering and crying, just as Loucan reached him.

He snatched the little boy up, thumped him hard on the back several times with the heel of his hand and brought forth more spluttering and a belch of seawater. The older children stood back, a little startled by the sudden arrival of a strange man in their midst.

Then their father emerged from between the mangrove trees that lined the edge of the water. He had a red, sunburned face and a belligerent attitude.

"What're you doing with my kid? Put him down!"

The child was still crying. Lass had almost reached the scene now, and she could see that the father had a point. Loucan's dramatic swoop and scoop had frightened the little boy more than the seawater closing over his head.

Apparently Loucan didn't agree.

"He could have drowned." His voice was hard with anger and emotion. "The older ones were playing. No one was watching him. A young child can panic or hit his head and drown in an inch of water in less than three minutes, quite silently."

"He's fine," the father insisted.

"Yes, because I reached him in time."

"It wasn't your problem. I was watching him. He sat up on his own. You're scaring him." He took the boy in his arms and attempted to stare Loucan down.

It didn't work. The merman simply stood his ground and said quietly, "I'm sorry if you think that I saw danger where none existed. I was thinking of the child's safety, that's all. Let's go, Lass."

She nodded. "Sure."

She thought Loucan was fully in control until she looked sideways, as they walked away, and discovered that his fisted hands were shaking. Then she looked closer. His mouth was a tight line and he was frowning heavily. The rolled legs of his dark pants were drenched to the thigh and his shirt was plastered to his body by the seawater that had streamed from the crying toddler. Loucan barely seemed to notice, let alone care. He was striding through the water, now just ankle deep and—oh Lord!

"Loucan, you've cut your foot," Lass said on a hiss of breath. She felt dizzy and sick at once.

He stopped to look down at his foot, and the spreading cloud of blood darkened in the shallow water. "I don't feel it yet."

Play the
"LAS VEGAS"
GAME
GET 3 FREE GIFTS!
FREE GIFTS!
FREE GIFTS!
FREE GIFTS!
TURN THE PAGE TO PLAY!
Details inside!

1. Pull back all 3 tabs on the card at right. Then check the claim chart to see what we have for you — 2 FREE BOOKS and a gift — ALL YOURS! ALL FREE!
2. Send back this card and you'll receive brand-new Silhouette Romance® novels. These books have a cover price of $3.99 each in the U.S. and $4.50 each in Canada, but they are yours to keep absolutely free.
3. There's no catch. You're under no obligation to buy anything. We charge nothing — ZERO — for your first shipment. And you don't have to make any minimum number of purchases — not even one!
4. The fact is, thousands of readers enjoy receiving their books by mail from the Silhouette Reader Service™. They enjoy the convenience of home delivery...they like getting the best new novels at discount prices, BEFORE they're available in stores...and they love their *Heart to Heart* newsletter featuring author news, horoscopes, recipes, book reviews and much more!
5. We hope that after receiving your free books you'll want to remain a subscriber. But the choice is yours — to continue or cancel, any time at all! So why not take us up on our invitation, with no risk of any kind. You'll be glad you did!

Visit us online at
www.eHarlequin.com

The Silhouette Reader Service™ — Here's how it works:

Accepting your 2 free books and gift places you under no obligation to buy anything. You may keep the books and gift and return the shipping statement marked "cancel." If you do not cancel, about a month later we'll send you 6 additional novels and bill you just $3.34 each in the U.S., or $3.80 each in Canada, plus 25¢ shipping & handling per book ar applicable taxes if any.* That's the complete price and — compared to cover prices of $3.99 each in the U.S. and $4.50 each in Canada — it's quite a bargain! You may cancel at any time, but if you choose to continue, every month we'll senc you 6 more books, which you may either purchase at the discount price or return to us and cancel your subscription.

*Terms and prices subject to change without notice. Sales tax applicable in N.Y. Canadian residents will be charged applicable provincial taxes and GST.

"It must be deep. It's right on your heel. You will feel it when the sand gets into it. There's so much blood...."

So much blood.

Lass felt sick and panic-stricken as her mind filled with the stark, familiar image of pristine, translucent turquoise seawater stained and polluted with dark red blood, thinning as it spread, and turning the water pinkish-brown.

Her mother, Queen Wailele's, death.

Ironically, it had been the first day in months that Lass had spent with her frail mother. They'd gone out together, just the two of them, to swim among the coral and the bright tropical fish on the nearby undersea reefs. They'd had no goal, other than to enjoy the beauty and each other's company.

Lass, always a bold explorer, had swum ahead, out of her mother's sight. She hadn't even known about the attack until she'd swum back in search of her mother, and found Galen's hired henchman holding his knife to Wailele's throat.

Lass had hidden behind a rock, too frozen with shock to move. Galen's thug had pulled her mother's body out of sight along the submerged reef, holding its lifeless shape the way lifeguards on Australian beaches held the swimmers they rescued from drowning. He'd disappeared, never knowing about Lass. She'd stayed, still unable to move until that pinkish cloud drifted toward her in the water like a ghost. Only then had she fled.

To Cyria.

She fled again now, blindly, away from the stain that was moving toward her feet.

"Lass! Thalassa!"

Loucan followed her, but she ignored him. The direction she took wasn't logical. She should have run to the sand and up into the safety of the barbecue area beneath the trees, with its grass and people and the smells of cooking food.

Instead, she went instinctively toward the open sea. It was only about twenty yards to the place where the current pouring out to sea transformed the sandy floor of the tidal lake into a narrow channel more than ten feet deep. Loucan was slowed by the cut on his foot, which had to be hurting by now. She was well ahead of him.

She ran until the water reached her thighs, then launched herself full length and began to swim, letting herself get carried by the current until she met the clean, churning foam of the breaking waves. She felt her tail begin to form, wriggled out of her panties, left them behind and kept swimming, needing the movement and the distance.

The power of the memory was beginning to ebb, but she knew Loucan would have questions. He would want her to tell him what was wrong, and she didn't know if she could. Didn't even know if she wanted to try.

When the membrane thickened fully, she dived beneath the waves without waiting for the slightly slower opening of the feathery gills in her neck. She'd trained herself to hold her breath for a long time. The sudden trebling of her speed through the water came as a huge relief. It was kin, she had always assumed, to what land people felt when they put on flippers or a fiberglass fin, but much more powerful.

The cold, clear water streaked past her skin, and the black dress she still wore seemed like a maddening impediment. Wriggling and stretching her body in the water, she pulled it over her head and left it behind to float slowly down to the sea floor or wash ashore in the next high tide.

Clothing always seemed so foolish and unimportant to her when she was in mer form. Even her black lace bra was a tight, uncomfortable impediment, so she shed that, too.

But she'd forgotten how much faster Loucan would be, and shedding her clothing had slowed her down. Loucan had been faster in freeing himself of his. Surging to the surface to breathe, she felt his hand close around her wrist.

"What happened?" he said. He sounded breathless from his impatience to reach her. "The blood made you panic. Why?"

"I can't talk about this."

Nausea rose in her gut once more, and she tore herself away from his grip, even though she knew he would follow her.

Loucan didn't let her get far, and this time he held her more strongly. His arms wrapped around her waist, then slid higher to her shoulder blades. She tried to keep swimming, but he matched her pace, his body undulating against hers in the same rhythm.

"You can talk about it," he urged her. "You have to. It haunts you, Lass."

Yes, that was how it felt—a ghost that appeared whenever she was most vulnerable. She slowed in the water and stopped fighting him, because she was too busy facing and fighting the demon of her memory.

"I'm right, aren't I?" he said. "This is the thing that haunts you. More than loneliness. More than the fear that someone will find out you're mer. This is why you're afraid, on a deep, subconscious level that you can't control, to go back to Pacifica."

The moment Loucan saw Lass's eyes, he knew he was right. In the light of the newly risen and nearly full moon, her pupils were dark, and whatever she saw in her vision, it wasn't him, even though she was only inches from him and staring in the direction of his face.

He held her and waited, feeling how she shivered in his arms, but even more aware of her lushly female body enclosed there. He had abandoned his clothing just as she had, both of them responding to the same instinctive need to feel the water on their bare skin. Their nakedness removed what little protection he'd had against his growing desire for her. He ached to dip his head lower and taste her full mouth, to explore the shape of her back and the weight of her breasts, despite his vow not to kiss her again.

He knew that Lass was unaware of his body's response, and too tightly wound right now to feel the sensuality that was so strong and newly discovered inside her. Loucan held his own needs in check and urged her once more, "Tell me, Thalassa."

"I saw my mother die," she whispered. "I *saw* it, Loucan! I was hiding. He—the assassin, the murderer—never knew I was there. And her blood came toward me in the water. She was so frail and defenseless. The last person in the whole of Pacifica who would ever have fought back. What a despicable, cowardly act to choose my mother! It would have been more courageous to choose me, an eight-year-old child! If only I'd understood what was happening! But I didn't."

"How could you have understood? And what could you have done?"

"I told Cyria, and she made me promise never to say what I'd seen. She knew that it would endanger my own life. It was only a few days after that when we left Pacifica. My whole memory of Pacifica is clouded by what I saw, the same way that her blood clouded the water. I've never been able to—" She broke off, then continued, "Once before, I saw a little girl get an oyster shell cut in the inlet. I fainted on the sand."

Lass shook more violently than ever, so Loucan held her closer, stroked her bare back and kissed the top of her head, as if she were still the child she'd once been. "Oh, Lass," he said, "and you've kept this shut away."

"I didn't think I could say the words. There's been no one to say them to, Loucan." Her voice cracked. "No one. Cyria would never let me talk about it."

Lass began to cry wildly, and Loucan held her quite still in the water, flicking his tail every few seconds to keep them afloat. He knew she needed this, and that he shouldn't hurry it. She could cry for hours if that would help her to release the pent-up grief and fear.

But it was disturbing to discover how much he needed it, too—the touch of her skin against his, the chance to give her something instead of being constantly on the lookout for opportunities to take.

The giving wasn't much, just a little human warmth and comfort, a listening ear. As she'd said, there had been no one, until now. The taking, on the other hand, was enormous. He knew that his arrival in her life had taken away her whole safe, carefully created little world. Although it had to happen, he wished he had more to offer her in return.

Maybe he did, he finally decided, when her long storm of tears at last began to quiet. Maybe the best and most obvious thing was right here and already happening.

If he kept her in his arms and kissed her again.

"Lass," he whispered. "Lass..."

He began to stroke the wet hair back from her face. Her breathing was still jerky against his chest, and her shoulders were shaking. He caressed them until she relaxed, then used his fingers to smooth the stress lines from her forehead and from around her brilliant green eyes.

Only when she was completely calm did he narrow the gap between his mouth and hers. At the first brush of his lips, she gasped, pushed her hands against his chest and tried to swim away, but he wrapped his arms more tightly around her and held her back. Their moving tails collided, and Loucan felt the hard shape of the gold bangle on her wrist, as well. He hoped it was waterproof. She'd obviously forgotten all about it.

"Don't fight, Lass," he said. "Let me hold you for a little longer. Let me. We both want this."

She shook her head, pressed her lips tightly together, then said, "That's not enough."

"It is for now. I can't think beyond it. I can't think of anything else at all."

Chapter Six

Loucan's mouth touched Lass's again before he had finished speaking.

His lips were cold and wet and salty, like hers, but it took only a moment for their kiss to grow warm and sweet. Lass closed her eyes. At first, she hardly dared to do so, afraid that the memory of her mother's death would ambush her once again.

But it didn't, and maybe the touch of Loucan's mouth and the feel of his body against hers was the only thing in the world that could have kept the nightmare vision at bay.

"Loucan..." His name made the most delicious pouting, kissable shape in her mouth, so she said it again, and he sighed something back to her that she didn't catch.

She parted her lips to taste him more deeply, and felt the slow dance of his tongue against hers. Thrills of sensation ran through her like showers of sparks, and she began to follow the slow, graceful ripples of his tail with her own movements so that they became a dance, too.

Not a chaste dance, either. He could touch her intimately. She could feel his arousal. In calmer, warmer waters, they could have joined together fully as merman and mermaid.

And, oh, she wanted that!

Or her body did. Every inch of her skin was on fire, and deeper inside she was aching. When he touched her breasts, gently at first and then with increasing possession and pleasure, she arched back and gripped his hips with her hands convulsively, unconsciously pulling him closer. He went still, then shuddered and began to kiss her even more deeply.

"Yes, oh, yes," he said.

No longer able to stay above water, they sank together into depths that were now darkened by the fall of night. Somewhere not too far away, they heard the muffled, chugging sound of a boat's engine. Most likely it was a local fishing boat heading out from the harbor in hope of a nighttime catch. They had sunk out of sight just in time, and the close brush with discovery should have frightened Lass, only there wasn't room inside her for thoughts like that right now.

Her sense of taste was sharper in the sea, almost as acute as a dog's sense of smell. She'd always known that, but it had never meant much to her before. Now it did. Exploring Loucan with her mouth, she discovered the unique taste of his skin, a blend of exotic flavors that made her think of cinnamon and coconut.

Although his tail held no particular appeal to her senses, it was a part of him and therefore important.

The scales that would have glinted golden-brown in the sunlight felt smooth, and the muscle beneath was firm and supple, a more powerful version of her own mer form.

Breathing through gills now, neither of them needed air. She could kiss him forever. Nothing else seemed to matter but touch and taste…until suddenly she tasted blood. On land her mouth would never have been this sensitive, but underwater it was. The gash in his heel was now transformed into a wound near the soft, finned tip of his tail, and it was still bleeding into the water.

The memory of her mother flooded her mind again, more vivid than ever. It brought with it the rising panic she dreaded. When she fought Loucan off and began swimming again, she took him by surprise, but he soon caught up to her. This time, though, he didn't try to hold her or stop her, just took her hand in his and swam toward the water's surface. Breaking through into the air, they both began to breathe.

"Can you see the boat?" she asked him.

"I don't care. We'll dive again if it's anywhere close." Loucan kept moving through the water, swimming on his side. The light of the moon showed Lass the determination and certainty in his face. "We haven't finished with any of this," he said. "Not your memories, and not what we felt for each other just now."

"Where are you taking me?"

"To my boat, moored in the harbor, where we can be alone and safe, and can talk."

At the speed they moved, it didn't take long to turn into the quiet harbor and reach his boat. It was a sleek, sizable vessel, with a polished wooden deck, a powerful motor, a tall mast for sails, and comfortable cabins below.

On deck, Loucan poured cold, fresh water over their bodies. Not expecting it, Lass shivered and screamed.

"Didn't you know?" he asked. "This will speed up the transformation by several minutes."

"I'd never discovered that."

"But Cyria didn't tell you?" He leaned to his side and pulled two thick, dry towels out of a storage hatch built into the deck, and spread them in front of them.

"No." Lass stretched herself out on her stomach, with her torso raised on her elbows. "For the first few years we were in Australia, we never went near the sea, and by the time we did, I'd forgotten all but the basic fact of the transformation. Everything I know about it, I've found out for myself, by trial and error."

She paused, then added, "Mostly error."

He laughed, then looked at her more closely. "I keep forgetting how alone you've been. Worse, in a way, than Kai and Phoebe, who were raised to fear the sea and didn't even know they were mer."

"No, that would be worse," she said, shaking her head. "I can't imagine not having the sea in my life."

He kept watching her, and her self-consciousness grew once more. They were both still naked, and her skin was sensitized by the ocean's caress as well as by his touch. She'd made her need for him so apparent. He seemed to feel the same, but that couldn't mean nearly as much to an experienced man like him as it did to her.

"When you fought me off just now, it seemed like you were fighting off the sea itself," he said.

"No. Never that."

"Then what happened?"

"I could taste your blood. It's just panic, Loucan." She could feel that her voice was shaking, but couldn't do anything about it. "I hate it. I don't know how to get over it. Talking helped. It did, the way you said it would. But it wasn't enough."

She shivered as the cool breath of the night air blew across her skin.

"You're cold."

He pulled out another thick towel from the storage hatch and laid it over her. She rested her head on her arms and closed her eyes, swept by a familiar lassitude. Soon, when her tail membrane split and left just a few flaking scales, she knew from experience that she would be ravenous.

"I want to tell you something," Loucan said.

His voice was a low rumble in his strong chest. Lass opened her eyes sleepily and found that he'd moved closer. He didn't seem to feel the cold. His waist was covered but his back was bare and still glistening with a few last drops of moisture. She couldn't take her eyes off the rippling muscles, the smooth brown skin, the hard, flat spot in the small of his back and the rising curve of his backside.

Her sleepiness and lassitude fled, but she made herself remain still.

"Anything you want to tell me, Loucan. It's so good to be able to talk."

"What happened at the inlet with that little boy..." he began. "I probably shouldn't have gotten so angry."

She blinked, having almost forgotten the incident that had caused him to cut his foot. "It wasn't wrong of you to be concerned for that child's safety," she said.

"There's a reason for it, Lass." His voice broke a little. "You see, I had a son once."

"Had?"

Dear God, I don't want to have to tell her about this, Loucan thought.

But he knew he had to. Her eyes, which had been sleepy and half-closed a few moments ago, were now wide and huge. She knew from his tone, and that sudden crack in his voice, that this was important.

He took his time over it, knowing she needed to hear every detail. She didn't interrupt his tortured narrative at all, for a long time. That made it fractionally easier to put the story into words. All the same, the words were clumsy ones. How could they be anything but?

"I told you the other day about my marriage, and that I never told Tara I was mer."

The truth about who he was had dammed itself in the back of his throat a hundred times from when he first began to get serious about the Arizona rancher's daughter. There were so many times when he could have told her. Riding together, hanging out over a late night snack in the kitchen of her family's ranch.

But he'd been so young, then—not that that was an excuse he allowed himself. Just twenty when they were going out together. Twenty-one when they'd gotten married.

He was crazy in love with her. Impatient and selfish and foolish about it. With no patience for waiting. No wisdom, and nowhere near enough trust. He was so afraid that she'd laugh in disbelief, or that the reality of who he was would repel her. He had thought about taking her on a vacation to the sea and just letting the transformation happen right there in front of her.

But the possibility of losing her was too hard to contemplate. He'd sacrificed the truth for the sake of making her his.

Only, of course, with such a lie between them, she had never truly been his at all.

"She knew I was hiding something," he told Lass. "And that it was something important. It started to come between us like another person. This big, secret lie. This thing that I wouldn't tell her. She made all sorts of accusations. She started watching me, and she went through my things when she thought I wouldn't know. She read my mail and I accused her of violating my privacy. I tried to put the blame on her, but in reality it all came from me. I was the one who didn't trust her enough."

So they had separated. Painfully. After a huge fight.

He had left her family ranch. In fact, he'd left the whole state and gone to New York, taking on a whole new identity. He'd spent those two years as a bond trader, working in lower Manhattan. He hadn't tried to contact her, and he found out later that she hadn't tried to trace him.

They'd both been too angry, and too hurt.

"What I didn't know was that Tara was pregnant. She had a baby boy seven months after I last saw her."

"Seven months. Then she must have known about the baby, or at least suspected, before you left."

"Yes. She knew. Things were already so bad between us that she didn't want to tell me."

"What happened, Loucan?"

Lass knew this story wasn't going to have a happy

ending. Loucan could see it in her face. So he just said it. "Cody drowned. When he was twenty months old."

She gave a tiny moan, which almost brought him to tears.

Mastering himself, Loucan went on with the story. "He and Tara had gone for a visit to her sister, who had a swimming pool. It was the first time he'd seen such a big piece of beautiful blue water."

The pool had been fenced, but Cody had found a place where the boards had been loosened by the family's dog. He had managed to squeeze through.

Loucan coughed to try and clear the tight, painful constriction in his throat.

"I didn't find out until six months later, when I finally came back," he said. "If I'd told Tara who I was, if I hadn't tried to hide the truth from her and from myself—I mean, hell, what was I doing, marrying a woman who lived so far from the sea?—she would have known how strong his need for water could be."

"She didn't tell you she was pregnant. If she had—"

"No, Lass. I'm not going to put the blame on her. I should have told her. I should have had the courage to accept the risk that I might lose her. That's why I know that my father was right to believe that the mer must open ourselves up to the rest of the world, and that's why I know it has to be done carefully. It isn't going to be easy. It never could be. But it has to be done. When I realized that, I went straight back to Pacifica."

"A good while ago."

"Fifteen years. I was so afraid of losing Tara, but

because I didn't tell her, I lost her anyway, and we lost our son. She's okay now. As okay as it's possible to be. She has a good second marriage, with a couple of school-age kids, a boy and a girl."

"You're the one who isn't over it."

She was right, of course, but not quite in the way she thought.

"I never want to get over it," he told her. "It's a lesson I never want to forget. You *have* to do the hard things in life, Lass. The fact that it's hard is the reason you have to do it." He took a deep, careful breath. "I think if you ever want to be able to deal with the memory of seeing your mother die, you have to go back to Pacifica, the way I did."

He waited, half expecting her to be angry and to accuse him of steering the whole point of his painful story in this single-minded direction, but she didn't. She seemed to recognize that he wasn't trying to manipulate her, and he was glad of that.

"I want you to think about it," he said quickly. "I'm not asking you to make any kind of a decision now. But if you decide that you're ready, I'll take you there. You'll have my protection, if you want it."

She nodded. "I'll...uh, keep that in mind."

He reached out to curl his fingers around hers, and then they both lay silent and half dozing on the deck for more than half an hour.

"I'm hungry, Loucan," Lass said a little shyly.

She stretched her legs beneath the towel and felt the last of her scales slip away. Her toes wriggled like newborn kittens, and the movement felt delicious.

"Thought you might be," he said. "I always get that way, too. I've got food in the cabin."

"But no women's clothing, I don't suppose?"

"For just such frequent occasions as this one? When I have a naked mer woman stretched out on my deck? No, I'm afraid not."

"Well, you might have," she said. "You keep this boat somewhere near Pacifica, right?"

"Not near, exactly. Hawaii, mostly. Not far if you know the right current at the right depth."

"And there are mermaids in Pacifica, as I remember."

"If you're asking whether I'm involved with a woman there, the answer is no." There was a forbidding look on his face and Lass flushed a little. "With the political situation, it hasn't been a priority. As for clothes, I can lend you a clean pair of boxer shorts and a T-shirt."

"That'll do fine." Too fine, possibly. Even the idea of feeling his clothes against her skin made something coil and ripple inside her.

"And I can cook us some steak and potatoes with a salad on the side."

"Even better."

Lass looked away quickly as he stood up, but not quite quickly enough. She still saw everything a woman needed to see. Loucan was so casual about his body. Didn't pick up the towel he could have slung around his waist, just padded down the steps to the cabin in his bare feet.

And he left the door open. Feeling like a schoolgirl for whom biology class wasn't nearly informative enough, Lass peeked. It was dark in the cabin for a few seconds, and she could see only a glow of blue-white moonlight outlining his arm and shoulder. Then he switched on a warm yellow lamp and began to move back and forth around the cabin as he opened various hatches and storage bins.

Each time, Lass caught a half-second flash of his body and absorbed a different impression. First, the shallow S curve of his spine as he reached for something stored at head level, then the long, hard lines of his thigh muscles, ending in tight knees, and finally the heavy darkness at his groin.

She heard the sounds of a gas flame being lit, and of steak beginning to sizzle in a pan. A microwave oven purred. There were some flashes of color—denim-blue and cotton-white—then he appeared again, clothed in jeans and a T-shirt, holding the clothing he'd found for her. She waited until he had gone back inside, then peeled off the towel and stood up to dress.

The harbor was dark and silent. It must be very late by now. Most of the commercial fishing boats were out at sea, and the pleasure boats had sails furled or canvas canopies fastened. Beside the farthest dock, one boat had its lights on and there was music playing. Some people were having a party on board, but they wouldn't be able to see this far.

Lass brushed some tiny, pearlescent scales from her legs, then slipped the boxer shorts on. They were made of silk, and barely perceptible against her skin, lighter than the caress of Loucan's fingers. The T-shirt was thicker and heavier. As she pulled it over her head, something dragged against the sleeve and squeezed her upper forearm.

Cyria's bangle watch.

Lass's stomach sank. She'd forgotten, hours ago, that she was even wearing it, and it wasn't waterproof like the other much more practical watch she wore most days, on the same wrist. She gave a little cry of consternation, and Loucan heard it as he came back up on deck.

"We can eat the hot meal in a couple of minutes," he said. "But I thought you might like a glass of wine and some cheese and crackers. What's the matter?"

"My watch." She fumbled with the clasp, trying to get it off. "I shouldn't have gotten it wet."

"Here, let me help."

The heels of his hands brushed her wrists, and his fingers were warm. With his head bent as he tried to work the mechanism of the clasp, his eyes were shaded by thick black lashes.

"It's stopped," Lass said. "The hands have stopped at eight thirty-five. That must have been when I first put it underwater."

"There, I've got it." He dangled the watch in his fingers and they both saw a drop of water seep from the back of the casing and fall to the deck below.

"It's ruined," Lass said. She felt sick with regret that she'd forgotten it. "That's... just terrible. I've looked after it so carefully for so long. Cyria always said that one day she'd tell me what the gift meant, but I didn't need her to do that. I always knew it meant that she loved me, and now it's broken."

"What it meant?" Loucan echoed her words. "She told you it meant something?"

"That she loved me," Lass repeated. "She could never say it, you see."

"No, Lass. It's more than that. I'm sure it is." He began to mutter under his breath. "It's tight. There's no screw or catch. I know nothing about jewelry like this. What have I got? A knife blade?"

"The key," she realized aloud. "You think this is where she's hidden the key."

"It's the right size."

"Why didn't she tell me? She would have *told* me!"

"She was waiting until she considered you fully adult."

"She died quite suddenly of heart failure, just a few months before I turned twenty-one. But Loucan, this is just an idea."

"That's why I'm looking for a razor blade, and a pocket knife. Hell, the steaks are burning!"

"I'll get them. You look at the watch."

Lass switched off the gas, then came back and watched as Loucan tried first his pocket knife and then a razor blade. Finally, with a tiny click, the back of the watch flipped open. More water dripped out, and beneath it was the quarter circle that Loucan had been looking for, its silver-white shape set into a circle of gold.

"I knew you must have it," Loucan said. "I should have guessed that Cyria would have it hidden in plain sight, and that she would have chosen a hiding place that was valuable in itself, befitting your status as a princess. It fits, too, that she wouldn't have trusted you with the knowledge until you were twenty-one, or maybe even older."

His blue eyes gleamed and he didn't even look at Lass. Her stomach dropped, and the closeness she'd felt to him so recently evaporated like morning mist on the water.

"You'll go back now, won't you?" she said, forcing her voice to stay steady. "As soon as you can.

This was the most important reason why you came. To find the final piece of the key."

He looked up, his expression clearer and more open than she had expected. "I told you that."

And you also told me that you'd take me to Pacifica, when I was ready.

Just minutes ago, she had trusted that promise. Now she realized that there was a corollary condition that he hadn't troubled to mention out loud.

As long as I'm ready when it's convenient for him.

"Take me home," she said. "To my place."

He narrowed his eyes. "Now?"

"Yes."

"Because you think you're not important anymore, now that I have the final piece of the key?"

"That's true, isn't it?"

"You were never important."

It was a brutal statement, and she gasped.

"Don't take that the wrong way," he cautioned.

She laughed. "Oh, there's a right way to take it?"

"*You* were never important," he repeated much more gently. "How could you be—you, Lass, the person you are—when I didn't know you? You've become very important, in such a short time. It rocked me to discover that we both had similar demons in our past."

"Yes," she agreed.

"Loved ones that we'd lost in a horrific way, and whom we both felt we should have saved. But don't ask me to solve that for you, Lass. Don't ask me to deal with it for you. You're the only one who can do that."

"You said—"

"Yes, I'll help you. I'll take you to Pacifica, if you

want to go. But you're the one who has to decide if it's the right thing, and if you can do it. And even though I might want to, I can't wait for long. Your accusation was right. This isn't about you. Or about me. It's not personal. In that sense, neither of us is important.

"It's about the safety and future of Pacifica itself, and all who live there. I'm not going to soften that truth for your benefit, Lass. I have the final part of the key now, and I'll leave here at first light, the day after tomorrow, whether you're with me or not. Now, are you going to eat, and have some wine?"

"Please." She thought she might pass out if she didn't.

"Good," he said.

"Why are you so blunt, sometimes?"

"Do you have to ask, after everything we've talked about tonight?"

"No. No, I suppose I don't."

He turned and went down the steps into the cabin without saying anything more. He was a man who made decisions and acted on them, she realized. A man who saw a problem, worked to find its solution, then put the solution into place.

She found it both refreshing and hard to take, like an unexpected splash of icy water in her face.

"We'll eat on the deck," he said. "I like it up here. I never spend much time below, unless the weather is bad."

He poured cold white wine into a glass and handed it to her. From the far side of the little harbor, there came the sound of voices and car doors banging as the party on the other boat broke up. The sea breeze had freshened, and the steak smelled salty and delicious.

"Forget the cheese and crackers," Lass said. "I'm too hungry to wait."

She took a gulp of the wine and began to eat, feeling a strange sense of giddy happiness that combined both exhilaration and peace.

Courage, too. Everything seemed simple, suddenly. Everything seemed *possible.* Before the feeling faded, she raised her glass once more, looked Loucan steadily in the eye and told him, "I will come to Pacifica with you. You're right. I'll never be at peace with my memories and with who I am, if I don't."

He nodded, then a smile of satisfaction spread slowly across his face, lighting it up with warmth. "I hoped you would," he said. "I had faith that you would. Can you be ready in time?"

"Megan, Susie and Rob will take over for me. They've offered several times to buy the place if I ever want to sell. But at this stage, I—I'm not sure how long I want to stay away."

"For a while, I hope..."

"We'll see."

"...because there's one more thing I wanted to suggest, Lass."

"Yes?"

"I want you to come to Pacifica as my bride."

For several seconds the words didn't make any sense. His bride? Was that what he had said? He'd also said that he was leaving at first light, a day and a half from now. That meant he wanted her to marry him *tomorrow?*

"You can't be serious!" she gasped at last.

"It's not about love," Loucan said quickly, before

Lass could gather her wits to find a better reply. "That's meaningless. I'm not even sure it exists."

"You loved Tara."

"I *wanted* her," he corrected Lass. "And to a young man cut off from his roots, that meant the whole package. I called it love, then."

"So what is it about?"

"Ensuring your safety. Strengthening the promise of unity in Pacifica. If Galen's son can marry Okeana's daughter, then people will see that there's hope for peace and compromise and change."

"This is another one of those times when you're not going to waste your energy on softening the truth, right?" she drawled. Her skin was prickling with heat and her lungs didn't seem to be working properly.

"Should I?"

He came toward her, took the wineglass from her hand and placed it on the deck. Suddenly, all her awareness of him, all her *wanting*—to use the word he'd chosen a few moments ago—was back, and they both knew it. He touched her cheek and looked into her eyes. Maybe she should have pulled away, but she couldn't.

"Shouldn't we build on this, Lass?" he asked her. His mouth was very close to hers now. "It's not love, but as long as we don't kid ourselves about that, does it matter? We both want peace for Pacifica. We want you and your siblings to be able to visit there in safety. Or even live there. And we respect each other. Those are very worthwhile things on which to build a marriage."

"A lasting marriage? Loucan—"

"Not if that sounds too hard. We can arrange a traditional mer ceremony tomorrow, and if it doesn't work out, you can have its protection while you're in Pacifica and still return here as a free woman. A mer marriage can't bind you legally on land. You have nothing to lose, Lass…"

Except my heart.

"…and everything to gain."

She nodded, ignoring the stricken little voice that had cried out inside her. "That's true."

And when she told him a few moments later that she would become his bride, she didn't know if it was the best and bravest thing she'd ever done, or the biggest mistake of her life.

Chapter Seven

She took his breath away.

Loucan was already waiting for Lass on the beach at sunset the following evening. They had chosen the quietest cove she could think of, accessible by car only with the use of Susie and Rob's four-wheel drive. The surprised couple had agreed to act as witnesses to what Lass had told them was a "personal commitment ceremony." Lass had explained that it was not a marriage, but something she and Loucan wanted to do to affirm their feelings for each other. In Pacifica, of course, it would be considered a legal and binding marriage.

Loucan had returned his rental car earlier in the day and walked to the cove, a good three miles along sand and around rocky headlands from the harbor at Condy's Bay. He'd arrived a little early, and he felt nervous in a way that a king embarking on a cool-headed political alliance should not.

He paced the hard sand just above the waterline in

his bare feet, already dressed in his mer wedding clothes of full-sleeved silk shirt and calf-length pants made of butter-soft sealskin. At last he heard the sound of the four-wheel drive engine grinding along the final section of the rough track. Several minutes later, Lass arrived on the sand, with Rob and Susie walking on either side of her.

And for a good thirty seconds and more, Loucan really couldn't breathe. He hadn't felt this way since those crazy early days with Tara. Young men were like that, though. A pretty face or a sexy walk could send their heads spinning for days. This light-headed feeling of suffocating awareness was all the more powerful because a mature man in his prime shouldn't still be able to feel this way.

Bearded Rob looked solemn, while small, freckle-faced Susie was grinning excitedly. She and Lass each carried bouquets of jasmine and white roses, which they must have picked from Lass's garden. Loucan vaguely took in Susie's outfit of blue and black, and registered that Rob wore something dark, but the only person he really saw was Lass.

She wore a white bikini, covered from the waist down by a diaphanous silver-white sarong that fell in soft folds around her bare, silky-smooth legs. A veil in the same fabric swirled lightly around her in the sea breeze, brushing first across her breast and then her shoulder.

She had white flowers in her hair, and several long strands of priceless Pacifican pearls around her neck. Loucan had given them to her this morning and asked her to wear them. At the time, the gift had merely felt appropriate. Now, the way the pearls gleamed on her body seemed like a brand of almost reverent possession. These treasures of the sea might be beyond price, but still their value was nothing compared to Lass's unique worth.

She was a bride fit for a king.

Her skin glowed pale gold against the white of fabric, flowers and pearls, and every curve of her body was lush and female and perfect. Like his, her feet were bare, and she'd painted her dainty toenails with a pearlescent polish. Even the way she trod the soft sand spoke of the sensuality at the heart of her.

Loucan felt a heaviness building in his groin and realized silently, *We never talked about tonight. Our wedding night. I don't want to consummate this. It would complicate things too much. It wouldn't be fair. But I never told her that. I don't know what she expects. And I don't know how strong I can be.*

Too late to do anything about it now.

She had almost reached him, and he could see the series of complex emotions shifting on her face, the way sunlight and shadow shifted on the ocean when the weather was changing. She looked shy, determined, eager and nervous all at the same time.

She was expecting a wedding night, with all that it usually meant. He could see it written right there in her face.

Dear Lord, why hadn't he said something, spelled it out? For his own protection as much as hers.

He was awed by the fact that she was prepared to entrust him with the innocence she'd been forced to keep for so long, but he didn't want it. Was it the responsibility he was rejecting? Or the power? He knew he didn't want to hurt her, but there was more to it than that—much more than he had time to analyze right now.

She was afraid. He could see that, too. And yet she didn't hesitate as she came to meet him. Passing her flowers to Susie, she held out her hands, and Loucan took them. They felt warm and soft and dry. She smiled up at him, the spread of her lips tremulous and slow.

"Hi," he whispered. "You look fabulous. Just perfect."

Why was his voice refusing to function properly? It was the same when Rob gave them the gold-rimmed white cards on which they'd handwritten their traditional mer vows.

Loucan had spoken vows of marriage before, to a giggling young bride in a Las Vegas wedding chapel. This felt so different. With the goals of their marriage clearly spelled out, this ceremony should have meant less than the one he'd had with Tara, but that wasn't how it felt.

Instead, the vows he exchanged with Lass were solemn and almost holy—not promises to disregard or carelessly break. Vows to fulfill, then? How far?

As he said the last word, Loucan knew that however much he held back, he'd already gone far deeper into this than he wanted to be.

Listening to the words on Loucan's lips, Lass found them beautiful and awe-inspiring. She had been the one to ask about them, just as she'd asked him about what mer brides usually wore. She had no memory of ever attending a mer wedding as a child. Loucan had confirmed that, yes, there were some traditional vows, and told her that mer brides were usually very lightly dressed.

He'd been a witness to numerous mer weddings in recent years, apparently. Some of them had been clandestine events, he had said, taking place between two people who'd grown up on opposite sides of the conflict that plagued the tiny undersea nation. It had taken only a few minutes for him to remember the words and scribble them down. And sure, yes, he'd said, he had no problem with saying them.

Today, he seemed less sure about it. His voice was scratchy and hesitant, and his lips hardly moved. Yet he didn't look down at the card he held for prompting. Instead, his blue eyes never left her face.

He must be nervous, too, she decided to herself. *He's humbled by this, just as I am.*

The full moon had risen over the water, and the sun had set. A lacy wave washed their bare feet then retreated again. Lass repeated the vows that Loucan had made, and that was the end of it. This was all they had planned. They were married now.

Still with hands joined, they looked at each other, lost in the moment, until Rob finally said heartily, "Aren't you going to kiss the bride, Luke?"

"That's right," Loucan murmured. "I'd forgotten that bit."

He frowned and bent his head. Lass closed her eyes and lifted her face, but it was over in a moment, just a light brush of his parted lips across hers. She opened her eyes. Loucan stepped back, still frowning.

There was a beat of silence, then Susie began to clap and cheer. She pulled handfuls of rose and jasmine petals from her bouquet and threw them into the air. The light breeze caught them at once and showered them onto Lass and Loucan. A couple of them settled on his silk-covered shoulder, and one landed on her cheek.

Seeing his hand reaching for it, she quickly brushed it away and turned to Susie and Rob.

"Thank you so much for doing this...."

"Oh, Lass, we were honored! A little surprised, but very honored," Susie answered. "And we will run that place like clockwork for you while you're on your honeymoon. Stay away as long as you like! What happens now? Can we drive you back to Luke's boat? I guess you'll want to be alone as soon as possible...."

"We'll walk back, shall we, Lass?" Loucan said.

"That's fine," she agreed, still trying to work out what she felt about that pale excuse for a kiss. "A walk along the beach would be...so romantic." The last words were mainly for Susie's benefit.

Susie frowned. "It's a long way. Too far for me! What is it about you two? You seem to belong here in a way I've never seen in anyone before." Her frown deepened, and a faraway light came into her brown eyes. "I could almost imagine that as soon as Rob and I turn our backs, you'll both dive into the water and—" She broke off, laughing, and shook her head as if to clear water-clogged ears.

"Susie?" Rob said curiously.

"No, it's nothing. Forget it. It's impossible. Ridiculous. A wonderful fantasy, but quite impossible."

Still smiling broadly, she opened her arms and gave Lass a huge hug. "I love the way you've done this," she said. "So original, with those lovely vows you made up. So private and personal. We went for the big family wedding, didn't we, Rob?"

"No choice," he answered. "We've both got big families."

"Which we loved, of course. But there was something really...'' Susie shook her head and ran her fingers through her hair, as though she'd walked through a spiderweb. ''...so *special* about this, with the ocean and the beach and the moon, and just the two of you.'' She kissed Lass, who had tears in her eyes now.

''I do have a good friend in you, don't I?'' Lass said to her.

Susie's brown eyes widened as she held her at arm's length. ''Well, of course you do, Lass Morgan!'' she said. ''Didn't you know that?''

''I do now.''

A few minutes later, Susie and Rob had gone, and Lass and Loucan were alone on the beach.

''I knew you would look beautiful,'' he said.

''Thank you.'' She felt the heat rising in her face.

''But the reality turned my expectations to dust. You look beyond beautiful. Thank you for agreeing to do this. I know it wasn't an easy decision for you. I'll do my best to ensure that you have no reason for regret.''

It was an oddly formal speech from a man to his new bride. Lass frowned at him.

He answered her unspoken question at once. ''I realized we should have been clearer with each other yesterday about what this entails,'' he said. ''I'm not intending for us to consummate this marriage, Lass. I don't want either of us to lose sight of what it's really about.''

She bristled. ''Would that happen if we slept together? And are you suggesting that I'm the one who wouldn't manage to keep things in perspective?''

''Both of us,'' he growled. ''Both of us would have a problem with that. You know that's true. Don't ever think I don't feel what you're feeling. This desire, this need that's growing between us. It's just as strong in me as it is in you. But I don't want the distraction. Wanting each other like this doesn't mean anything. Not when there's so much else that's more important."

Hard to argue with that.

Lass felt selfish and trivial for even thinking about their wedding night in personal terms. She understood exactly where his single-mindedness came from, and wondered if she understood better than he did how much it had to do with his personal past. She didn't like his rationalizations, nor his choices.

Do we have to choose between Pacifica and our own needs? Isn't there room for both?

One look at the hard set of his face made her keep those questions to herself. She might desire him, respond to him as a woman in a way she'd never known she could respond to a man, but this didn't mean she would blind herself to the streak of cool-headed ruthlessness woven deep into the fabric of his nature.

She was stronger than that.

"Look," he said, cutting across her increasingly confident train of thought. "There are the dolphins..."

She followed his pointing hand and saw two dark, curved fins loop gracefully out of the water and disappear once more. With her eyes fixed on the moonlit ocean, she counted seven of them. They were surfing. The fishing must have been good, they'd eaten their fill and now they were ready to play.

They streaked through the curve of each breaking wave, then dived down and out of sight at the last moment, only to reappear back out to sea, ready for the next one. They jockeyed for the best position, appeared to tease and chase each other, and all of it was pure play.

Lass laughed. "I love them when they're in this mood."

"Maybe we could get ourselves in that mood, too. There's no one else on the beach, Lass."

Tonight she didn't need anything more in the way of encouragement, and they definitely needed a distraction from each other. Wading into the water as far as her thighs, she felt the sarong dragging around her legs. Her veil was wet, too. She pulled it off uncertainly, then found that Loucan had brought a woven sea-grass bag for their clothing. He wore its long strap across his bare torso as they swam.

This time, she kept the protection of her bikini top, and they surfed with the dolphins for an hour. The mer transformation happened seamlessly, without guilt or fear, the way she dimly remembered it happening in her childhood, and her feelings about Loucan were so confused that the waves seemed steady by comparison.

If he wasn't here, I couldn't feel this same joy, she thought. *And yet he's turned my life upside down. I can see that it had to happen. In some ways, I can't imagine a better messenger from my childhood. I want him so much, but it's not a blissful feeling. He's not making any of this easy for me, and there's a hardness to him. Could he ever be a safe man for a woman to love? I doubt it. I'd be afraid to love a man like him....*

A dolphin's sleek gray body arrowed past her and veered across her path. Turning to avoid it, she collided with Loucan himself and felt his strong hands clasp her waist, keeping them both steady in the water. With one ripple of his body, he'd swum away again, leaving every inch of her skin newly painted with sensation. Breaking the water's surface, she had to gasp for air.

It was another two hours before she and Loucan finally hauled themselves, breathless, onto the deck of the *Ondina*.

Lass had filled a large hatch with her things earlier in the day, so this time she had clothing to wear. As the night was sultry and still milky warm, and her skin was still reluctant to endure the touch of fabric after the liquid caress of the ocean, she chose a pair of brief denim shorts and left her white and almost dry bikini top in place.

She was a little too conscious of how brief the bikini was, conscious of the way her breasts jutted and the way the thin straps defined her shoulders, but knew she would only draw attention to the fact if she changed.

Loucan wore shorts, too, and a chambray shirt with the sleeves cut off at the shoulder seam. That just emphasized the powerful shape of his upper arms, and Lass found it hard to look away.

"Hungry?" he asked her casually, but for once she wasn't.

Her emotions were too raw tonight, and had translated into a churning feeling in her stomach. As Loucan had planned, they would leave the harbor tomorrow morning at first light, and it would take them around ten days to reach Pacifica.

Ten days with Loucan on this boat.

The sleek craft wasn't nearly big enough. And maybe Lass was wiser than he was in this way.

Maybe it was the very fact that she was so inexperienced compared to him. She could see the truth more simply and clearly.

They would end up sleeping together.

"I'm not hungry yet, but you eat," she told him. "Please don't wait." Her heart was jumping wildly in her chest. "I'm just going to sit out here for a bit."

And try to work out how I'm going to handle this.

"Go ahead," he answered.

He disappeared inside the cabin. Lass sat deliberately with her legs dangling over the stern of the boat so that she had her back to him. A few minutes later, she smelled bacon frying and heard it sizzling in the pan.

I could wait, she thought. *I've waited long enough! Within a day or two, the tension between us will be so tight it'll snap with one accidental touch, and how can we avoid that on a boat? He talked about distractions, but wanting each other like this and tying ourselves in knots to stop it from happening would be the biggest distraction of all.*

Instead, she could make things easier for both of them.

I could seduce him tonight.

If she dared.

Just the thought of it made flames lick inside her, made her crazy heart jump harder, and filled her with such a mixture of longing and terror that she could hardly breathe. The growing heaviness in the air didn't help, and a few minutes later, she heard thunder. She looked beyond the lights of the harborside town and saw a flash of sheet lightning against the treetops.

Within five minutes, crashing rain had driven her

into the cabin. Loucan looked up from the scrambled egg he was scooping onto slices of toast. "Getting a little damp out there?"

"Just a bit."

The temperature had dropped, too, and the rain had started so suddenly that she was already half-wet. She shivered, and knew that the convulsive movement would draw his gaze to the flimsy bikini top. Her nipples were hard from the cold, and when she hugged her arms around herself, the gesture lifted her breasts and made them look fuller.

He didn't say anything.

The cabin itself was warm and cozy. Far too cozy, just as she'd known it would be. When she sat down opposite him at the table, she felt his bare knees brush hers. Once more, she saw ten days on this boat stretching ahead of her. Ten days of trying not to touch each other. Ten days of their bodies filling the same small space. Ten days of eating together, and knowing he was sleeping in a bunk bed just one thin wall away from hers.

Loucan was kidding himself. Big time.

"The rain's stopped. I might see if—"

"I'm going to check our mooring. Just in case it's gotten—"

They spoke and moved at the same time, and collided midsentence. His arms shot out to her elbows to steady them both, and his deck shoe came down hard on her bare toes. She gave a hiss of pain and bent to grab her throbbing foot just as he looked down to see if he'd done any serious damage. Their foreheads cracked together, and Lass saw several pretty yellow stars.

"I'm sorry," she gasped.

"My fault. I'm really sorry. Are you okay?"

He was still holding her, and her body was drawn to his like a magnet. Earlier, out on the deck, she had believed that there was a decision to be made. She'd thought she would have to take her courage in her hands. But when it happened, it wasn't like that. Instead, it was so easy and obvious that there simply wasn't any other choice.

Looking up at him, she reached for his neck and slid her fingers around to his nape in a caress that was slow and tantalizing and deliberate. A little shaky, too, if she was honest.

She said softly, "I'm fine, Loucan. I'm feeling no pain."

And then she pulled him closer and kissed him.

At first, his mouth didn't move. Lass brought her other hand up to his face and rested both palms lightly against his jaw. Her lips soft and slightly parted, she tilted her face a little and printed her kisses with slow, purposeful pressure. He tasted salty and warm and perfect, and she couldn't imagine wanting to be anywhere else in the world but in his arms.

His hands responded to her sooner than his mouth. She felt them curve over the bare skin just above the waistband of her shorts. They were impatient hands, not content to rest. He pulled her hips against him and only then, at last, did he start kissing her back.

Sweet relief flooded through her, and a sense of confidence and triumph that made her dizzy. What would she have done if he'd somehow found the strength to push her away?

"Lass," she heard him mutter. "I don't think I can...I don't want—"

"If you think for one second," she said fiercely,

"that we can stop this—that I'm going to *let* you stop this—you're so wrong! I dare you to even try. I dare you to tell me it's even possible!"

She was right.

With every eager, inviting touch of her mouth on his, Loucan knew it more fully. Ten days on a boat. Virginal Lass showing in her body everything she felt and everything she wanted. He would hardly be a man if he didn't respond. That stuff he'd said to her after their wedding ceremony a few hours ago was total nonsense. They would both burst into flames if this need went unconsummated, when by mer custom and law it was their full right to do so.

"Teach me, Loucan," she whispered. "Help me, and show me what to do. Reading about it, imagining it…that's not the same. I need you to show me."

"Yes. Oh, yes!" His words were just a rasping of breath across her mouth.

The thought of catching her up on fifteen years of inexperience might have daunted him. Instead, it made his blood sing in his veins. Ten days wasn't the endless interval he'd considered it a few minutes ago, it was the blink of an eye. Nowhere near enough time to give Lass what she deserved.

And as for tonight…

For a long time he just kissed her, slowly deepening the joining of his mouth with hers. He lifted his hands to her breasts, touching them softly through the stretchy fabric of her bikini top, tracing his finger around the low-cut neckline. He touched her through her shorts, as well. Laying his palm over the mound at the joining of her thighs, he could feel her rising heat.

Her skin was incredibly sensitive. Her breathing

was already fast and shallow with pleasure and need, and when he unfastened the clip at the back of her top and took her fully into his hands, she gasped.

And this time, she recognized his own state of arousal at once. Hands on his hips, she moved so that their thighs were locked together. She began to rock her hips, tentatively at first. It drove him wild, and when he told her so, she laughed, kissed him harder and rocked more sinuously.

He tasted salt and wetness on her cheeks. Dear heaven, was she crying?

She was.

Good tears.

He pulled away far enough to look at her, and found that she wasn't ashamed of them. She was smiling at the same time. "Don't stop," she said.

"You were right," he muttered. "I couldn't if I tried."

"Let me touch you."

She reached for his shirt and unfastened the first two buttons, then he helped her pull it impatiently over his head. Two more buttons snapped off. Loucan stood motionless as she ran her hands over the muscles of his shoulders and back and chest. Her eagerness heated his own blood still further, and he ached to feel the pressure of those full, tightly peaked breasts against his body.

Hearing a fishing boat coming by, he reached out and shut off the cabin light. With a full moon still rising in the sky and washing its blue light in through the cabin windows, they could see each other clearly. That was important. For her, too, he could tell. Her green eyes had darkened and she wasn't ashamed of her pleasure in watching him.

She wanted his eyes on her, too. Her body spoke this fact more clearly than any words. She didn't try to hide the lush responsiveness of her breasts, and when he brushed his fingers lightly over her nipples, she closed her eyes and dropped her head back and moaned.

"Let me see you. Let me touch you," she said a few minutes later, and Loucan felt her hands working at the front of his shorts.

He helped her, and in a moment he was naked and she could see—and feel—exactly how aroused he was.

He swallowed hard. Almost any other woman of her age would have known what to do. Lass didn't. She wasn't thinking about results, she was just exploring, and that was far more erotic than he could have imagined. Her fingers were tentative, curious, delicate, and when they left him after a timeless interval, he wanted them back. What was she doing?

Taking off her own shorts. And she wore nothing underneath.

"Lass," he croaked. "Here?"

"Saves moving."

"But—"

Pushing with her hands, she lifted her bottom onto the edge of the table, then stretched her arms back and braced them behind her so that her breasts jutted more invitingly than ever.

She knew it, too. She knew exactly how full and lush and touchable she looked, every inch of her. At the same time, she was blushing and he loved that. *Loved* it. Oh, he'd suspected—*known*—how sensual and responsive she would be, but he hadn't expected her to lead the way like this, with such a captivating combination of daring and nerves.

"Not like that," he told her, through the tightness in his throat. "Sit up. Right on the edge. Let me—"

"No, Loucan," she whispered. Her arms wound around his neck. "Show me," she begged him. "Don't tell me."

"Show you?" he repeated. "Oh, yes, I'll show you all night long."

She wasn't leading anymore. Neither of them had the patience for that. He held her thighs as she wrapped them around him and they both disappeared into a world with no time, no words, nothing but their two bodies moving together.

It was two in the morning before either of them slept, entwined together on a bunk bed that should have seemed way too narrow for two. Loucan's last waking thought was that he never wanted to let her go.

Chapter Eight

When Lass woke up, the boat was already moving. She could feel the subtle vibration of the engine and the shallow rocking motion of the hull in the water. She lay there for a moment, her body still replete and pleasurably aching with the aftermath of Loucan's lovemaking.

There was no regret. Not for what they'd done, nor for the fact that she'd made most of the moves. Loucan had liked that. She was certain of it. She could still see the hot light of appreciation in his eyes, still feel on her skin the way he'd taken hold of the intimacy she'd begun to create, and powered it to a tumultuous finish.

More than once.

She should be feeling exhausted. Instead, she felt alive and bursting with energy. Rolling from the bunk bed, she wrapped herself untidily in the striped sheet and went to the adjoining cabin to find some clothes.

The tiny porthole showed that dawn was barely beginning to color the eastern sky. In the darkness, she was too impatient to spend long looking for the right garments, and contented herself with a black bikini, hip-hugging white shorts and a stretch cotton sweater with a pattern of tiny red flowers.

When she reached the deck and came up to Loucan at the wheel, they were just leaving the narrow mouth of the harbor. The sky was getting brighter, but there was a mist on the water, and it was cold.

He put his arm around her shoulders at once and kissed her, his mouth tender and slow. "Ready for this?" he said.

"Yes," she promised carelessly.

She wasn't thinking very far ahead. At the moment, feeling as she did the way they fit so perfectly together, nothing seemed impossible, as long as he was with her. The boat seemed to float across the water, and Loucan's touch turned her bones to sweet whipped cream.

He kept his arm in place around her waist, and she leaned against him, content to watch the way he controlled the boat with such confidence, the way it cut through the waves, and the way the sun rose and burned away the morning mist.

"Want some breakfast?" he said eventually.

"Love some," she answered. "You can go below deck, of course, can't you? I don't know much about boats. You can set it on cruise control, or something, right?"

"Or something, yes." He grinned. "Have you got something in mind for me to do instead?"

"Well, breakfast, like you mentioned, and then..."

"Yes?"

"You've got some books on hand, I noticed. And a couple of, uh, games we could play."

"Monopoly or Scrabble might be nice," he agreed.

They both knew he was teasing her. Finally she collapsed into laughter. *Literally* collapsed. Laughter, on top of the whipped cream feeling in her limbs, made all her joints begin to buckle. But Loucan held her up and kissed the strength back into her body, and they didn't get down to breakfast for another hour....

Tomorrow.

With the cooperation of ocean and weather, they would reach Pacifica tomorrow, Loucan knew. He wished that some freak tropical storm would brew up and blow them a thousand miles off course. Alternatively, a shipwreck would be good. They could swim together to the nearest uninhabited island paradise and wait to be rescued. If no one ever came for them, because no one knew where they were—a little detail that he could take care of—there'd be no complaints from him.

He and Lass had just spent the most incredible nine days together. The summer weather had cooperated fully, sending the right winds their way. They'd spent most of the journey under sail, and he'd had to use the motor only a few times to increase their speed when the wind dropped overnight. He'd taken advantage of the currents he knew so well, and they'd moved faster than any commercial vessel could.

They'd called in at a couple of ports on the way, to restock supplies of food, fuel and water. Both times they'd used it as an excuse to relax a little, exploring the environs of the port, browsing in a few stores and then stopping to eat at a pretty restaurant overlooking the water.

Any other couple would have called it a honeymoon.

Loucan didn't dare.

He suspected how close Lass had gotten to falling in love with him. He knew that, for her sake, he should be doing everything he could to prevent it happening. Instead, he watched it growing inside her, the way he sometimes watched storms building at sea.

It was a beautiful sight, Lass Morgan falling in love. It made her eyes brighter and her mouth softer. It made her aware of her own body. Sometimes, she seemed to get an attack of shyness, and he loved the way she would hug a sheet up to her chin, or make him turn his back while she washed herself up on deck. At other times, she was as bold as brass, and would anoint her naked body in moisturizing sunscreen and lie in the sun for hours, knowing he couldn't help watching her.

They ate picnic meals on deck, or drank hot chocolate in the cabin late at night, and talked about a hundred different things, and he got to know her better than he'd known any woman except Tara, so long ago.

No, better than Tara, too, he decided. Because there was more honesty between him and Lass than he'd ever permitted himself during his marriage.

The one thing he hadn't been honest about was the way he felt.

He couldn't love her.

Maybe she didn't realize yet that she wanted him to, but soon she would. Loucan held traditional views in that respect. An emotional woman like Lass couldn't give herself to a man for the first time, make love to him over the course of ten passionate days and keep her heart free. A man found it easier to do so. Loucan desired Lass, respected her, wanted only the best for her, but he couldn't love her.

He couldn't afford to.

He had to keep his head and his heart clear in order to know what was best for Pacifica. He had to stay focused. The closer they got, the more the needs and problems of his country began to weigh on him. The alliance he'd made with Lass had political, not personal, goals, and it would be dangerous to both of them if he forgot the fact.

It felt as if he'd been away for a long time, and he began to question his own decision to handle his quest for Thalassa this way. Once he had found her, should he have tackled the whole thing more directly? More brutally? Should he have just kidnapped her and headed for Pacifica at full speed? He'd wasted more than a week on gaining her trust and overcoming her fears.

And he could have made this journey in eight days, not ten, if he'd pulled out all the stops. Instead, he'd lingered those two times on shore, loving the way she responded to the exotic cultures of Fiji and Tahiti, deliberately delaying their journey to give her pleasure.

Within a day of my meeting her, she'd gotten to me more than I intended, he thought, watching her. *How did I let it happen, when I started out so cool and so clear about my goals?*

It was late in the day, and once more she was stretched on her stomach on the deck, no clothes in sight, lazily turning her skin to a gorgeous honey-gold. One look at her and he wanted her, and a moment later, when she stretched and rolled onto her back, lifted her head and smiled at him, it was all he could do to keep standing at the wheel.

"Hi, Captain," she said softly.

His hands tightened on the curved piece of chrome and he didn't return her smile. His anger at himself was building every moment. The time had come to get this whole thing back under his control. He checked his navigation charts and adjusted the boat's course, noting figures for latitude and longitude that were getting closer and closer to those of Pacifica.

Behind him, the sun had begun to drop into the ocean with a speed that told him they were near the Equator. Only in higher latitudes were sunsets a lengthy phenomenon. Tomorrow, at around eight or nine in the morning, they would arrive at the tiny, uninhabited atoll where he could, in a pinch, leave his boat in safety for several weeks. From there, an hour or two of swimming would bring them to the secret kingdom of Pacifica.

A dozen questions jostled for prime position in his mind. Where was Joran right now? Whose side was the man claiming to be on at the moment? And how many people in Pacifica understood, as Loucan himself did, that Joran was only out for his own gain? Was it safe to tell Phoebe, Kai and Saegar to come visit, with their new partners?

"Is anything wrong, Loucan?" Lass asked.

"No, everything's fine," he lied. "Just checking our new course." He forced himself not to look at her, and picked up his train of thought from where it left off.

Lass hadn't yet handed over her section of the key.

Not that they'd talked about the key much. He hadn't actually asked her for it. When he did, how complete would her trust turn out to be?

She must realize that Kai and Phoebe and Saegar had had an easier decision when they'd given him theirs. For each of them, it wasn't about putting the final piece in place. The seal that opened the door to the treasure of Pacifican scientific knowledge could only operate with all four pieces in place. If Lass didn't give him her key, however, he'd have to write off half the purpose of this trip, and his claim to be the best leader for his nation would be far less strong. Unless he entrusted the decision about the key to her.

Meanwhile, in Pacifica, anything could be happening.

"I could get us something to nibble on before we start dinner," she offered.

"I'm not hungry, but have something if you want." He made the words as casual and cool as he could.

Her face fell. She was so sweetly easy to read. She wanted him in bed. Or maybe just a chance to kiss and talk and make each other laugh. Both of them had gotten very good at all of those things.

Maybe he shouldn't be so hard on himself, Loucan decided.

He'd married her, and they'd consummated their vows. If anything could make a woman trust a man, it was that. A couple of months ago, if anyone had asked him, he'd have said he'd be open to sleeping with the unknown Thalassa for this reason alone. A pregnancy would be a convenient bonus, as well.

Now, he had to struggle to remind himself that he was so directed, so cold-blooded. He hoped, too, that there was no baby growing inside her. He didn't want to bind her to him or to Pacifica in that way.

"Show me Pacifica on the map," she said, after a moment of silence.

"It's not on the map," he growled. "This is a map made by people who don't know Pacifica exists."

"Okay, so show me where on the map Pacifica would be, if people knew it existed," she said patiently.

There was no edge to her voice, and Loucan knew he was being unreasonable. Being something he wouldn't even say out loud in her hearing, because she had such a sweet, clean mouth and almost never cursed or swore.

"Here," he said. "Southeast of Hawaii."

He made a tiny crescent on the chart with his thumbnail, and she leaned closer to look at the spot. She smelled like ice cream and sunscreen and salt, and the bare arm that brushed against him was hot from the sun and dewy-soft from the moisturizing cream she'd applied. The little detail of her nakedness was hard to ignore, under the circumstances, but he did his best.

"And right now, we're here." He made another mark on the chart, only this time his thumbnail slipped and instead of a tiny indentation, there was a hole. He swore under his breath—again—and tried to smooth down the triangular tear with little success.

"That's close," she said. "Isn't it?"

"Tomorrow morning, we'll leave the boat," he answered. "We'll reach Pacifica by lunchtime, swimming the last twenty miles across the coral reefs."

He caught her sharp intake of breath, and remembered that she and her mother had been swimming the reefs together when Wailele was killed. Hardening his heart, he pretended not to notice that Lass was fighting the memory, and didn't give her the support she probably wanted. She was strong enough. She would handle it.

"I think I'm getting burned," she said, after another interval of silence. "I'm going to get dressed."

"Lass…" Her name slipped out without him wanting it to.

"Mmm?"

"Never mind."

With a tiny shrug and an even smaller smile, she disappeared below deck. When she came back a few minutes later, she was dressed in light cotton pants and one of those snug-fitting T-shirts that left him in no doubt as to what her body did to him.

"*Now* can you talk?" she said immediately. "Don't pretend you don't know what I mean."

"That you distract me incredibly when you're naked? I didn't think you needed me to tell you that again."

Her face tightened, and her voice was deceptively calm and sweet. "I just asked you, Loucan, not to pretend. Something's changed. When you looked at the navigational chart and saw how close we were to Pacifica. Even before that." Her voice grew husky, but she fought her tears, won the battle and went on. "Something…just changed."

How much was he prepared to hurt her? Loucan wondered. *When* was he prepared to hurt her? Now, deliberately, when at least she'd have the chance to get over it with some privacy? Or later, in Pacifica, when he wouldn't have to tell her anything? She would discover all on her own just how little time he had for her when there were more important concerns that took precedence.

The second choice might save him an awkward scene, but at the same time it would leave Lass even more vulnerable.

Now. It had to be now.

He at least owed her that, after the way they'd spent the past nine days. It rocked him to discover how attuned they had become to each other's words and moods. She'd picked up on the subtle signs of his changing focus, and he had no trouble now seeing her wind her emotions in tighter and tighter coils.

"Nothing's changed," he said, as cool as he could be. "The honeymoon's over, that's all. When we reach Pacifica, you'll have a certain part to play as my new bride. Public appearances, in which it's vital for us to show our united commitment to peace. But in private, I won't have much time for you. Not the way we've had on the boat."

"I wasn't expecting that you would! Or that *I* would!"

"I'm not just talking about time. I'm talking about emotional focus. This marriage was a political strategy, but I think we're both in danger of forgetting that."

"Oh, so you're actually reminding me not to do anything silly like fall in love with you?"

"Something like that."

"Isn't it a little arrogant of you to assume that such a reminder is necessary?"

"Arrogance is a fault I've been accused of before."

"I'll bet it is!" Her control broke like a dam across a flooded river, and her anger gushed out in full spate. It was a magnificent sight, though Loucan didn't want to dwell on the fact. "And you think *you're* in control enough to keep your body's needs separate from the involvement of your heart, but I'm not?" she said.

"No, Lass, I—"

"Oh, right, *right!* I get it!" She huffed out an indignant laugh. "You're so fabulous in bed that any woman—especially a virgin—who gets a taste of your performance is going to be your love-slave for life. Good one, Loucan!" Her sarcastic praise bit hard. "I guess it goes with the territory. A man who is arrogant enough to believe that he can lead an entire nation out of twenty-five years of sporadic, destructive war is going to have no trouble believing every woman he meets is secretly pining for him."

"You haven't—"

"And since I've been very open about wanting you, I must be totally desperate. It couldn't possibly be that there was something very magic and important about acknowledging my female desires after so long. Because let me tell you something. You don't know me or understand me nearly as well as you think you do, King Loucan! *I am so angry with you*!"

Without giving him a chance to reply, she whirled around and vanished into the cabin.

"That went well," Loucan muttered.

His hands were gripping the wheel so hard his knuckles had turned a sickly green. The back of his neck felt ready to snap with tension. He was willing to bet that she'd never had an outburst like that in her life. For a woman who'd kept her emotions so cool and controlled for so long, it was pretty impressive.

Impressive enough to raise some serious questions.

Most importantly, did she mean it? She was such a unique combination of strength and vulnerability, and he didn't know which quality he'd just witnessed. Her vulnerability? Was lashing out simply a way of hiding how much he'd hurt her? Or had he just seen proof of her strength? Maybe she was right. Maybe it was pure arrogance to suggest that her sensual response to him would bring with it an emotional involvement too deep for him to match.

Loucan couldn't remember when he'd last been this uncertain about something so important.

Below deck, Lass was talking to the mirror.

"So, Lass Morgan, is this a learning curve, or a descent down a very slippery slope?"

Thirty-three years old, and she'd never lashed out at anyone this way before.

It felt... She paused to consider.

Embarrassing? No. Sad? Absolutely not.

It felt fabulous. She was tingling all over, hot-cheeked, alive, *angry* at Loucan and extremely pleased that she'd told him so.

But people got angry at the ones they loved. Was she in love with him?

How could she know? She had no way to make comparisons. It would have been very easy to let herself float along in a cloud of rapture. Loucan could make all the decisions and all the moves. Loucan was strong, brave, intelligent, trustworthy. Loucan did wonderful things to her body, and sheltered her in his arms afterward as if she were a lost lamb. At his side, she need never think or struggle or work or doubt again.

"But Cyria didn't raise you that way," she told the pink-cheeked, glittery-eyed Lass in the mirror.

For all Cyria's faults, she'd never encouraged Lass

to be weak or dependent on anyone. It wasn't something Lass intended to experience now.

Going to the boat's small galley, she tossed some garlic and fresh shrimp in a pan with melted butter, found the last packet of pasta in one of the storage hatches beneath the bench seats and put a pot of water on to boil. Although they'd added to their food supplies with fresh treats from the sea, their stocks were getting low.

"Pacifica." Lass tried the word on her tongue. "Tomorrow we'll be in Pacifica."

It didn't seem possible. Pacifica was hardly a real place to her anymore. Instead, it was a combination of random memories like snatches of film, some of them wonderful, others disturbing. She would have remembered more, she was sure, if the most nightmarish memory of all hadn't haunted her so much. For twenty-five years, she hadn't *wanted* to remember Pacifica in any way.

Now, for the first time, she tried to bring the images back.

The palace. There was a palace, only her own royal clan were not the only people who lived there. In her memory, it resembled a luxurious shopping mall, with a warren of concourses and atriums, hundreds of suites of rooms and miraculous displays of color and light.

And there were gardens, weren't there? Farm gardens, which still grew some of the earth-dependent foods that the ancient Pacificans had prized. She had the idea that those foods were getting rarer, that this was part of the old knowledge that her father had kept under his own control and hidden away. Did it really make sense to treat knowledge as a commodity? Or as a weapon? Wouldn't it ease tensions between the different factions if it could be available to everyone?

Caves. She remembered caves, too—some of them as luxuriously fitted as wealthy homes on land, others more primitive, and distant from the central palace.

Lass drained the cooked pasta and tossed it with the shrimp and garlic sauce, then went up to Loucan on deck. She was tempted to stand there, far away from him, with her arms folded and a dagger-sharp look on her face, but she overcame such a petty reaction and moved close.

"I've cooked dinner." She touched her hand briefly to his forearm as she spoke, and felt the sun's heat on his skin, and the fine golden silk of sun-bleached hair. "Pasta and the last of the shrimp we caught this morning. Can you come below and eat? Because I have some questions."

He flashed her a sharp glance, in which she was sure she detected a glint of curiosity and respect. Damn straight, he should respect her! He could be curious, too, if he liked. There was nothing mysterious about this.

"About Pacifica," she added. "I want to know what it's like there now."

He nodded. "Yes. You're right. You need to, don't you?"

"I should have asked you days ago." But even so recently, she hadn't had the courage. Now, suddenly, she did. And she had an announcement to make, as well. She wasn't going to give Loucan the key, until she'd thought more about how the archives in her father's secret chamber should be used.

* * *

Loucan held Lass's hand as they crossed the coral reefs.

For the first ten or fifteen miles, they were stunningly beautiful, an unbroken, shimmering mass of color and movement. Lit by the strong rays of the tropical sun, the water was a pure, translucent aquamarine. It was like swimming through liquid gemstones.

At first, Lass found it impossible to believe that this paradise was the setting for the nightmare that had haunted her for twenty-five years, but then they reached a place where the color and composition of the rocks changed, and there were several barren stretches where the coral had been destroyed.

With her heart beating faster, Lass turned to Loucan and asked, "What happened here? It's so ugly!"

Only when she'd said it did she realize that she hadn't spoken any words. She'd *signed* to him. It was the way the mer communicated underwater. She hadn't thought about it in twenty-five years, but now, when she needed it, and as her memories were activated by the growing familiarity of what she saw, it had come back.

"The fighting," Loucan signed to her in reply. "The guerilla elements of both factions have adapted the mer technology for creating energy out of phosphorus. They use it for explosives now."

Last night, he'd told her about the sporadic outbursts of fighting. It resembled what she'd read and seen on the news about the troubles in Ireland, with each side taking revenge against the other side's violence until many people lost sight of the original grievance.

Last night, he had also entrusted her with all four sections of Okeana's key.

"You're right. You must be the one to break the seal," he'd told her. "With me beside you. Until the right moment comes, no one will know you're in possession of the key. Few people in Pacifica even know it exists, or understand the value of what your father locked away."

"Joran does."

"Yes, unfortunately. Hide it in your bag of belongings when we leave the boat, and find a secret place for it once we've housed you safely in Pacifica. We'll both know the right moment, I think, when we must go together to unlock the seal."

Lass hadn't been fully compliant on this point. She'd left two parts of the key on Loucan's boat. The others she carried in the woven sea-grass bag that trailed beside her in the water as they swam.

A little farther on, Lass recognized the place, just ahead, where the reef ended and the water suddenly became much deeper. Almost home. There was a back entrance to the vast labyrinth of the air-filled palace just near here, with rooms where the mer would rest while they shed their tails. This was where, as a child, she would often begin to think of something to eat, and toys and stories and bed.

Now, as then, she might be less than a day away from seeing Saegar and the twins. A radio message they'd received last night on Loucan's boat communicated that they were on another boat heading here from Hawaii.

Her anticipation crowded out bad memories as the familiar stretches of coral passed beneath her. *I've done it,* she realized. *I've swum across the reefs with-*

out panicking and falling apart. I've rediscovered the beauty of it, instead of the terror. This was where I first learned to love beauty. My mother taught me, and it has stayed with me despite everything that happened after. Her death wasn't the only legacy I took when I left Pacifica. When I see the beauty of the mountains behind my house, or the perfect shape of a ceramic bowl, it comes from what she taught me.

Lass felt as if she'd just found some very precious possession she had thought was lost forever.

A moment later, Loucan slowed, and she realized there were some shadowy figures in the water just ahead. Mermen. Several of them, and a couple of mermaids as well. They made a sign that meant nothing to her, but Loucan clearly recognized it.

"They're friends," he signed to her. "A patrol. But I'm surprised they're this far out. I would have expected to find them closer to our headquarters."

It was so strange to be surrounded by other mer. The signing between them and Loucan was fast and fluent, and Lass had no hope of following it. When they began swimming rapidly through the water as a group, she had to ask him, "What's going on?"

"Problems," he explained. "And a disappointment for you, I'm sorry to say. You won't see your siblings here, after all. Or at least, not yet. They're waiting on their boat until it's safer. The patrol leader, Carrag, has been in touch with them. He's been a supporter of mine for a long time, and he's advising us to go cautiously as well, but I'm not sending a message like that to those who believe in me. I won't be frightened away from Pacifica."

"Nor me," Lass answered at once. "Not anymore.'' She knew the words pleased him, although he said nothing. ''But why isn't it safe now?'' she asked.

''Joran has taken over part of the palace—Okeana's former throne room and the suite of rooms surrounding it. From a strategic perspective, that's not very clever of him, as it's a hard place to defend, but symbolically it's important, and he knows that. Effectively, he's declared victory. He's broken both of the pretended alliances he's made with each of the other factions over the years, and gone out openly on his own. He's got supporters, but hopefully not as many as he thinks. Joran dropping his cloak of charm and concern for Pacifica's good may unite the Swimmers and the Breathers in a way that nothing else could.''

He used the names for Okeana's faction and Galen's that Lass had almost forgotten about until he'd mentioned them last night. Still they meant very little to her.

''Meanwhile, Kai and Phoebe and Saegar aren't here,'' she signed. She couldn't immediately overcome her disappointment and drag her focus from the concrete, personal sense of loss to Loucan's far more objective and statesmanlike concern.

He gave a crooked smile at her forlorn, clumsy gestures, and signed to her, ''That's what you care about in all this? Your siblings?''

She didn't attempt to defend herself. ''Yes! The rest is too abstract for me right now. I don't even know where we're going. If Joran controls the palace—''

''A tiny part of it. You've probably forgotten how huge it is. For hundreds of years, it was the whole of Pacifica, and only once the process of mer transformation was fully understood and perfected did we start occupying or constructing air-filled undersea caves farther afield. That's where I'm headquartered, in a whole network of caves that we're heading toward now. When we get there, I'll need to go into council to talk about this new situation with Joran. Selkia and Nacre will look after you."

He gestured to indicate the two mermaids in the patrol group, then slowed and turned to look at Lass. For a moment, she thought he was going to say something more—something personal—with those strong yet surprisingly graceful hand movements she was quickly relearning. But in the end he only chopped them through the water in a gesture she didn't recognize, and swam quickly on.

Chapter Nine

The next few days passed in a jumble of new impressions and rediscovered memories.

Selkia and Nacre took their duty of looking after Lass very seriously. Both of them were strong, beautiful young mermaids with deep auburn hair that streamed behind them as they swam. They were sisters, it turned out, and Lass envied their easy, loving rapport.

She didn't understand half the jokes and teasing remarks they signed back and forth. It was a little easier once they entered the cave system where Loucan and his supporters had their headquarters. Like the palace, it was filled with air, which meant the mer could take on land form, wear the clothing that still resembled sailors' garb from long ago, and use spoken language instead of signing.

Selkia and Nacre spoke something like eighteenth century Cornish pirates, but Lass found their strong accents and odd vocabulary easier than the signing. There, it would take her a while to regain her full fluency.

Although she was pleased at the way everyone received her, it was daunting for Lass to discover how much she was the focus of everyone's hopes.

"The news of your marriage has disappointed half the unwed mermaids below the age of fifty," Nacre told her, at the end of her fourth day in Pacifica. The two of them were swimming lazily in mer form, in a shell-tiled saltwater pool heated by undersea volcanic gases. "And a few of the wed mermaids, as well! Not me," she added quickly. "Carrag and I will wed when next the moon is full. I am sure Loucan is the right man to bring peace, but I have never wanted his wooing."

She sounded very earnest, as if she was afraid Lass might distrust her intentions, so Lass said quickly, "I'm sure you haven't."

"They say Joran is biting his tongue in fury," Nacre continued. "He blames your alliance with Loucan for the fact that his supporters are deserting him. He does not realize that he has made so many enemies among both Swimmers and Breathers that everyone is uniting in the hope of bringing him down. And if," she added eagerly, "you should be carrying Loucan's child, that would be perfect."

"I'm not," Lass told her. She regretted it seconds later. Why hadn't she been a little more vague? Her answer would only encourage Nacre's questions.

"A pity," the other mermaid said. "He will have to come to you more often at night, if 'tis to happen."

"That's step one, yes," Lass drawled.

"But he has not come to you at all, has he?"

Plenty of times on the boat, Lass could have said,

but none since we got here. She contented herself with a simple, "No," then added, "he told me it would be like this."

Why was she defending him? Thinking back on the few times they'd been in each other's company during the past few days, she knew he could have found opportunities to connect with her. Just a private squeeze of her hand, a special look or a whispered phrase in her ear. Instead, he had barely glanced at her, and the smiles he'd given her were a public performance and didn't reach his deep blue eyes.

She should be furious about it, not hurting like this.

"Are men like that on land?" Nacre asked curiously.

"Some of them. The ones like Loucan who care more about politics than they do about people."

"Loucan does not. Not usually. He does what he believes is necessary."

"And so do I."

"In other words, if you cannot lie with him, you wait until you can. But you miss it. Badly. I know."

Lass didn't correct Nacre's interpretation of her words. The other mermaid said nothing for a minute, then spoke again.

"Selkia is part of a patrol group going out across the reefs tomorrow to contact your siblings. Loucan believes that it will be safe for them to come here now. Joran has not launched the attack we were all afraid of, once he set himself up in the palace. His garrison is not strong enough. The decision about coming here will be up to your siblings, of course. They may still choose to wait."

She went on talking about the strategic situation for a little longer, but Lass couldn't follow it. All she could think of was the news that Selkia was going to see Saegar and the twins.

Why can't I go, too, with the patrol group?

"Is there a chance that I'll see Loucan tonight?" she asked Nacre as soon as the other mermaid had stopped speaking.

Nacre laughed. "That is just what I was thinking about Carrag. 'Tis hard to long so much for a man!"

"I didn't mean—"

"Thalassa, I see your face when you look at him. I can send for him, if you like. I can have him told that you want him to come to you."

"Could you?"

She didn't care if Nacre and everyone else thought she was desperate to have Loucan in her bed. She didn't care if Loucan himself thought the same thing...or she tried not to care, anyway. She just wanted to see him and ask if it would be safe for her to go across the reefs with the patrol group to see her siblings.

Nacre promised to ensure that the message was delivered, and she must have kept her promise. Just before Lass went to bed, on a mattress of some downy stuff, covered in sheets made of a seaweed fiber that felt soft and cool like pure linen, an answering message came from Loucan. It was delivered by Nacre's own fiancé, Carrag.

Not tonight.

Nothing more. Just those two words.

"Loucan says to tell you, not tonight."

Lass was simply frustrated at first. The anger came a little later, when she'd spent a frantic twenty minutes thinking, *All I want is five minutes conver-*

sation with him, but how do I get to him? I have no idea where he is!

Nacre didn't know. She had relayed the message to Carrag, who'd told an older man who was also part of Loucan's inner circle. It was late, and the cave system was quiet. If mer technology had encompassed cell phones, Lass would have appreciated one right now, as well as a little mer mother-of-pearl PalmPilot with Loucan's phone number in it.

As matters stood, she had two choices. Let the whole thing go, and put off the longed-for meeting with her siblings yet again, or search for Loucan herself.

No. Wrong. There was a third option.

Why did she have to involve Loucan at all? If he couldn't find even a few snatched minutes of time for her, why shouldn't she simply bypass him? She knew where Selkia slept, right near an exit from the air-filled caves into the open sea. Lass could wait there and join Selkia's patrol group in the morning.

Not knowing how early they planned to set out, and with no way of ensuring that she'd wake in time, she abandoned her comfortable bed and stayed in the ocean all night, floating and dozing near the exit from the caves. It left her tired, but it worked.

The patrol group appeared just as the light of dawn began to penetrate the water. Selkia looked surprised when Lass swam in among them, but she signed quickly, "I want to see my siblings. Loucan believes it's safe."

It was as vague a word in mer signing as it was in spoken English, and that was convenient. She hadn't alerted them to the fact that Loucan had no idea she was here. They seemed to accept her presence, and as the morning light turned the water from dark jade to pale aquamarine, she crossed the coral reefs once more.

This wasn't the way she'd come from Loucan's boat, and she recognized only one distinctive outcropping of rock, which she must have seen once, long ago. The lifeless state of these reefs was far worse than the ones she'd swum across the other day, and she asked one of the mermen about it.

"Joran and the Swimmers joined battle against us here a few years ago," he explained. "We lost some good men, and so did they. Many of their side crossed to us after 'twas over. They told us Joran did not care how many lives were lost, nor what he did to the coral. Much of it, he blasted himself to make better defenses."

They swam on, and Lass had trouble keeping up. She hadn't realized it the other day, but Loucan must have been pacing himself to match her more limited speed.

"I wish he was here...." Something twisted uncomfortably in her stomach, and she suddenly ached to feel his touch, or just his strong presence beside her. No matter how hard she tried, her anger was always mixed with other more powerful feelings, where Loucan was concerned. It had been that way with him from the beginning.

Her muscles began to burn, and she felt a dangerous urge to breathe real air instead of filtering oxygen out of the water through her gills. Barely sleeping last night hadn't helped her energy levels, and it seemed hours before they began to swim up toward the sun's light.

When she broke the surface, the first thing she did

was draw in deep, panting lungfuls of air. The other mer turned away, as if she was doing something a little indecent, reminding her that there were nuances to mer etiquette and culture of which she still knew nothing. She swam away from the group in a slow circle, and when she'd rejoined them, she found that they had seen the boat they were looking for—the boat where Saegar, Phoebe and Kai were waiting.

It was a moment she would never forget.

With the boat's engine powering the craft toward them, she could soon see several figures on deck. The morning sun shone on two blond heads, one honey-colored, the other like silky straw.

"Phoebe and Kai," Lass whispered under her breath.

Both women wore colorful bikinis, and both stood beside tall men who looked well tanned from their days at sea. One of them was pulling up the zipper on a slick black wetsuit, while the other still had a pile of diving gear at his feet.

There were two more figures on the deck, as well—a man and a woman, already dressed in full scuba gear, with oxygen tanks on their backs and breathing masks ready to pull into position. They had to be Beth and Saegar. Her brother, who had forever lost his tail for the sake of living on land with the woman he loved…

All of them were studying the group of mer in the water. Lass and the five members of the patrol had now almost reached the hull.

"Loucan's not with you?" Saegar called out. Like Loucan, he had a deep, powerful voice.

"No," answered the patrol leader, who was

Nacre's fiancé, Carrag. "He's staying close to home, waiting for Joran's next move."

Lass saw the disappointment in her siblings' faces, and felt it in her own heart, as well. She had the sudden sense that it had been wrong of her—dangerous, even—to give in to her impatience to see Saegar and the twins without consulting Loucan. He should have been beside her at this moment. For a whole lot of reasons.

She hardened her heart. Maybe he could have spared her the five minutes she'd wanted last night, and then she'd have known if this was a foolish expedition for her to undertake. Or if—less likely—he might have wanted to be here with her at this moment for a more emotional reason.

She hadn't even seen him in almost two days.

"But we have Thalassa here," Carrag called up to the boat.

"Omigosh, *Lass?*" Kai squealed, as Lass waved. "Yes! I see you!"

She dove into the water and came up, her face and hair streaming with water, next to Lass. They hugged, cried, looked at each other and hugged again. Lass forgot about Loucan, and her odd sense of foreboding regret that he wasn't here.

Phoebe wasn't far behind her sister, and she was teary and emotional as well. Considering that the twins hadn't experienced their first mer transformation until just a few months ago, they both seemed amazingly at home in the water.

Saegar was awkward by contrast. "Don't laugh, big sister," he growled, after swooping at her and giving her a bearlike hug. "Legs still don't feel right in the water. Beth is teaching me how to move, and fortunately she's very good at it.''

Beth had swum up beside him, and when she wrapped her arms around him, they seemed like two playful seal pups in their black suits. She looked very pretty and young, with a warm fire of new love burning in her eyes.

Kevin and Ben had finished putting on their diving gear now, and joined their wives in the water.

''I couldn't find you,'' Kevin told Lass. ''But I wasn't surprised to hear that Loucan had succeeded. Sometimes you need intuition, not facts.''

''How long is the swim, Carrag?'' Saegar asked. ''Should we have brought the boat closer?''

''That's not safe,'' the merman answered. His accent wasn't as strong as Nacre's or Selkia's, and Lass guessed that he'd had more contact with land-dwellers, maybe as a result of Loucan's guidance. ''We never like to anchor a boat directly over Pacifica. In any case, the water's too deep there. You need a place like this, where the reef will hold the anchor, and where there's an atoll nearby to shelter the boat from storms.''

They talked about air tanks and flippers for a while, as well as hearing an update from Carrag on what was happening in Pacifica. Ben seemed very concerned for Kai's safety, and Lass wondered if he was always that protective. She couldn't imagine Loucan treating her that way. Was this part of the difference between love and mere attraction? Once again, she felt more alone than she wanted to be, without Loucan beside her.

I've been alone for more than thirteen years, since Cyria died. And I have Saegar and my sisters now, she berated herself inwardly. *What's wrong with me? I'm stronger than this, I know I am.*

The journey back across the reefs was magical at first. Unlike Lass, Kai and Phoebe had no memory of the place at all, and spent the long swim pointing in delight at the frenzy of brilliant colors. Saegar and Beth never left each other's side, and Lass knew that this experience must be hard for her brother. When you'd swum in mer form, scuba gear wasn't the same. Beth seemed to understand this instinctively, and Lass again found herself envying their closeness.

Fatigue enveloped her, and she began to drop back almost out of sight of the others, unable to keep up. Even Beth and Saegar had swum ahead, now.

I should be feeling so happy, but all I can do is wallow in feeling left out. That's not fair. In fact, it's pathetic! Do I really begrudge Saegar and my sisters their happiness?

She wouldn't, if Loucan was here.

If Loucan loved her. It was pointless to pretend to herself any longer that what she felt for him wasn't love, because she knew it was, even when she was angry with him!

Then, out of the corner of her eye, she saw a male mer figure swim out from behind a phosphorescent tangle of coral. For a few crucial seconds, she actually thought it was Loucan himself, and turned toward him, her heart full of eagerness. He must have been searching for her. He must have guessed where she'd gone. Oh, she wanted so much to tell him how she felt!

By the time she realized it was someone else, they'd almost collided. He was heading straight for her—not a big man, but wiry and as lithe and supple as an eel in the water. He snaked his arm around her, flipped over and lashed his tail back and forth so hard in order to gain speed that it whipped her own tail painfully, scratching like rose thorns.

She struggled to see his face, but it wasn't until he'd pulled her behind the outcrop of coral that she was able to do so, and even then, it wasn't until he signed to her that she recognized him.

"Sweet little princess, I knew it was you. And all grown up so beautifully."

"Joran..." She felt sick.

"You remember. I wondered."

"And *I* thought you were under siege in my father's throne room."

"Under siege?" His face twisted, and his signing was sharp and ugly. "Is that what Loucan is saying? I've claimed power, Thalassa. That's a very different thing. And when you've given me a particular key, which I know you have in your possession, my claim will stand without challenge."

"Do you think I'm going to hand over the key? Do you actually think I'm carrying it with me?"

"No, but you'll tell me where it is."

"I won't!"

"Stubborn! All right then, sweet little princess..."

She didn't bother to react, although she knew he wanted her to protest against the condescending phrase.

"...tell me what you'll do when I start to hurt you."

"His supporters are drifting away every day. I vote that we wait."

"And I say that we have to act. If we don't take

hold of this new unity between Swimmers and Breathers, it will disappear."

"If it's that fragile, it will disappear anyway," Loucan interjected. "I don't believe it *is* that fragile."

His head was pounding, and he'd grown increasingly frustrated by the hours of circular debate droning on in the council chamber. He was in favor of action, but not out of fear that unity would disappear. He knew that his own weariness reflected the mood of Pacifica's whole population.

There had been a generation of conflict and unrest. Families were divided, and some clans had scattered to primitive undersea cave dwellings, far from the once-beautiful labyrinth of the palace. More people wanted peace than ever before, and wanted it sincerely. It wouldn't take much to make Pacifica beautiful again. Only peace.

In his view, all that remained to decide was the moment and the method. Another pitched battle? No one wanted that. And yet if Joran was quietly overpowered and held for trial, or allowed to slink away, there would be no emotional moment of victory to cement the population's mood. He had the uneasy and growing feeling that if he didn't take the right action soon, he'd lose his chance.

He kept thinking of Lass, which helped nothing and no one. Lord, he'd get her out of his mind if he could!

He had brushed off her message last night. He'd regretted it immediately, yet still hadn't gone to her as she wanted. Dozens of times a day, he parried suggestive jokes and questions about the state of their married life. Was she pregnant? Was he having a good time trying to get her that way? Was this, truly, the political marriage he claimed it was? Would he, for example, have married her quite so quickly if she'd looked like a blowfish or a sea turtle?

"It's nothing to do with her looks," he had by this time, and very irritably, told at least fifteen people.

But it had to do with her looks, of course, and with everything else about her as well. He honestly couldn't have said anymore, whether she was beautiful, but she was beautiful to *him.* Her heart, her laugh, the successful life she'd made for herself on land, the strength she'd shown when he'd deliberately cooled off toward her on the boat.

She was fabulous, and he'd ignored her for two whole days, mainly out of guilt because she deserved so much more than the shallow marriage he'd given her.

"Let's adjourn," he told the council. "I need a break."

But when he went in search of Lass five minutes later, she was nowhere to be found.

Neither was Joran. Loucan had a spy in the merman's inner circle, who reported, "He's left the palace suite. No announcement or fuss, he just slipped out. He's got the place as strongly guarded as ever. Doesn't want anyone to know he's not there. What could be important enough to take him away?"

Swimming aimlessly toward the reefs, Loucan asked himself the same question. In the distance, he saw figures, and not all of them were mer. It must be Saegar and the twins, their spouses in scuba gear, and the patrol who had gone to meet with them.

That's where Lass is, he thought. *Of course! She would have heard that the patrol was going, and she wouldn't have wanted to risk not seeing her siblings if they decided to wait longer on the boat. Was that what her message was about last night? And could Joran have heard about the patrol, as well?*

Quickening his pace, he swam toward them, looking for her. The group was strung out, with Beth and Saegar swimming apart from the others, and Kai and Phoebe both staying close to their non-mer husbands. He couldn't see Lass.

Carrag had recognized him now. He swam ahead of the group, and the two of them met up. "Was Thalassa with you?" Loucan asked at once.

"Yes, she's..." Carrag twisted around. "Where is she?"

"You mean she *was* with you, the last time you thought to check. Unless she's way back, she's not with you now. Carrag, weren't you looking out for her?" Loucan felt ready to explode, but reined in the reaction, and ignored the painful pumping of his heart. Lass's safety was important. Castigating Carrag was not.

"No, don't waste time in explanations," he added quickly. "She was with you, for certain, until when?"

"We left the boat," Carrag reported. "We came back over the reefs. She began falling behind our patrol. I looked back a few times, but she was close to Saegar and Beth."

"Who are in another world right now, with eyes for no one but each other."

"I..." Carrag twisted his fingers together, turning his signs into garbled nonsense. Controlling himself, he added, "I'll come with you."

"No. I'll go alone." Loucan gave Carrag more instructions, then began to power through the water, sick at how much time had already passed since Lass was last seen. The weight of the ocean seemed to suffocate him, and for some reason he thought of Tara and their little lost son.

If I've made another mistake like that... I can't *lose her. I can't. Why have I been lying to myself about how important she is?*

She was with Joran. Loucan knew she was, and he knew what Joran wanted from her. Okeana's key. He doubted that Lass would give it to the renegade merman, and he was terrified that her courage might cost her her life.

"We should be safe here for long enough," Joran told Lass.

"Who should be safe? Not me!"

"Don't answer back like that. Your signs are as crude as a sailor's. You're a princess, Thalassa. If you hadn't so naively married Loucan, you might have had the chance to marry me. You'd have won back your father's throne. It will still be possible for you, once Loucan's death has widowed you."

"Share the throne with you? No, thanks."

"Then you accept that it is rightfully mine?"

"No. Did I give that impression? Sorry, you must have misunderstood!"

"You're making me angry, Thalassa."

Lass knew that. She was doing it on purpose, trying to distract him and buy herself time. Until she'd worked out a means of escape? Until her siblings noticed she was missing and raised the alarm? Her plan didn't go beyond that. Yet. But if she had time to think...

"And when I'm angry," Joran signed, "I sometimes lose control."

"Of what? What do you have control of in the first place?"

"I mean it. Stop wasting my time, and tell me where you've hidden the key, or I *will* hurt you, my beautiful future bride."

"Why is the key so important to you, Joran? Don't you believe you can keep power without it?"

"Sometimes the mer can be almost as shallow and misguided as land-dwellers are. If I can bring us back the prosperity and technology we used to have, a generation ago, I'll be Joran the Great, reigning over a golden age. That was my biggest mistake, advising your father to lock our treasured knowledge away. I never suspected he'd send his own children into exile with the keys. I thought he'd give them to me."

"Gee, bad luck!"

He raised his arm, and she ducked aside in a rippling motion. The blow caught her tail, where the top of her thigh would have been, and ripped the scales away painfully. He had sharp fingernails that were of a macabre length for a man.

Lass shuddered, and hoped he hadn't seen. She didn't want him to know that beneath her bravado, she could so easily be afraid of him... He had her imprisoned with him beneath this rocky ledge, too shallow to be called a cave, and now, from some hidden crevice, he'd brought out a knife, made of the same metal as the precious key he wanted.

He held it against her side, and said in a chatty voice, "Now that we're getting down to business, how long do you think before someone—Loucan, let's say, if he cares enough to look for you—will find you in this spot? Wouldn't it be much more sensible to tell me what I want to know, so we can get out of here together?''

''No. I won't tell you anything.''

Overcoming her rising panic, Lass forced her mind to work.

The ocean was very still here, and incredibly clear. If she could do something to cloud the water, it might serve as a signal. The section of reef Joran had chosen was badly damaged from the fighting, and some of the rock looked fractured and loose. If she could move it…

It wasn't the most brilliant plan, but at least it required action. She didn't wait any longer. Disguising her movements as a bid for escape, she lashed her tail wildly back and forth, and barged as hard as she could against the most fragile looking rock face. Joran grabbed her immediately and since she was so fatigued, he won the struggle almost at once.

Meanwhile, however, the rocks fell onto a ledge thickly covered with coral debris almost as fine as dust, and a cloud of it slowly began to rise and spread. Joran nudged the point of his knife into Lass's throat. ''Don't try that again. Take me to Loucan's headquarters and show me where you've hidden the key, or believe me, you *will* suffer.''

''Yes, all right,'' she signed, making her hands deliberately shaky. ''Give me a chance to rest for a few minutes first. I'm tired. I've already swum for miles today. I can see there's no hope of trying to fight you. You're so much stronger and smarter than I am.''

Would he buy her capitulation? Only if his ego was big enough. Apparently it was.

''Of course I'm stronger, sweet little princess,'' he

signed. "Strong enough to show some mercy to my future bride. I will expect you to remember that."

"Oh, I will, Joran..."

Lass slumped against the rock as if completely exhausted, and they waited. Joran's knife was still pricking her throat. He would use it, she was sure. And yet he'd talked casually about making her his bride. The contrast between this insane lack of logic and Loucan's reasoned talk with her on the boat about putting personal issues aside for Pacifica's sake suddenly made her see things in a new way.

I shouldn't be angry with Loucan. His priorities make sense, and I'm only being petty. Oh, if I could only tell him that, right now!

With images of Loucan filling her mind, she covertly watched the fine debris spreading and spreading in the water, not daring to accept that it was her only hope.

When Loucan saw the clouded water, he cursed it. How would he find Lass if he couldn't see? What had stirred up the debris like that? A fight? Occasionally, if two hotheaded young mermen from opposing factions met up, there could be violence. But he couldn't see anyone, and he couldn't see or taste blood.

Blood in the water, moving like a cloud.

Lass had talked about that, when she'd told him about secretly witnessing her mother's death.

Lass.

Had *she* created that cloud?

He swam fast and silently, hugging the shadows of the rocks. When he saw her, seconds later, his stomach gave a sickening twist. Joran was beside her. They were hidden beneath an overhanging rock, and neither of them had yet noticed his approach. She looked so limp. What had Joran done to her?

No, what have I *done?''* Loucan's thoughts were barely coherent. *I've treated her like a chess piece, not like a person. Did I really think that warning her in advance to expect such treatment was good enough? I should have* made *time for her. If Joran has hurt her...*

No. She was alive. Moving. There was no blood, but Joran had a knife.

Take him by surprise, Loucan coached himself. *Don't think this out for too long. Go with your gut.*

His sudden movement made the water seem to boil. Seeing Loucan a fraction of a second before he was tackled, Joran turned like an eel, his knife flashing in his hand.

''Swim, Lass.'' Loucan yelled the words, creating only a meaningless, muffled sound in the water. ''Get away.''

She understood, but she shook her head. She'd grabbed Joran's tail, but he was lashing it wildly, and she lost her grip. The powerful fin caught her across the face, drawing blood like a cat's claws, and she jerked sideways and sank to the ledge below. At the same time, Loucan went for the knife, but in the struggle both men lost it and it sank quickly out of sight. He didn't think it had gone far. Lass might have found it if she'd looked, but she was focusing her energy elsewhere.

Loucan didn't have time to work out what she was doing. Although Joran was smaller and less powerful, he was agile in the water, and very fast, and he used his tail as a weapon. Feeling the sting of it against his body, Loucan realized that Joran had pierced his tail fins with deadly metal barbs, the way people on land wore piercings as jewelry.

Joran had always worked that way, substituting cunning and trickery for what he lacked in overt strength. He might win this, if he drew enough of Loucan's blood....

No. *No.* And leave Lass in his hands? *No.* Joran would do anything for the key. Lass's life would be worth nothing.

And so would my life, if I lost her.

Loucan fought harder, willing himself to overcome the fatigue brought on by nights of sleeplessness. He felt Joran tiring, but those barbs were still doing their damage. He surged back against the rocks, readying himself for a decisive lunge, felt Lass pulling him sideways, then lost vision as the water churned and blurred with debris once more.

He glimpsed Joran, and readied himself to continue the fight. Couldn't understand, at first, why the other merman was thrashing his body like that, yet not coming any closer. Then he realized that Joran was trapped. The full thickness of his tail was wedged among the rock fall that Lass had triggered, unnoticed by either man in the frenzy of their fight.

Loucan felt Lass signing frantically beside him. There was blood in the water, but she ignored it.

"...didn't dare hope...go now, before he breaks free...want to use the key and make what's in my father's cave free to everyone in Pacifica...can't be used as a weapon like this...what I've decided to do."

"No," Loucan told her. "I'm not leaving him. It can't end like this. Our people need something decisive. Punishment."

"Exile." Joran was speaking and signing at the same time. "I choose exile."

"It's not your choice, Joran," Loucan said.

"Yes, it is. It *is*."

He had found the fallen knife among the debris, and they saw him stretch his arm out and just manage to clutch it. Immediately, he began slicing at his tail, going deep into the membrane with one long, fast, powerful cut from where the scales first formed to where they merged into his barbed fins.

Loucan felt Lass grip his arm. "He'll kill himself, cutting that deep. Won't he?" she signed in agitation.

"No, but he'll never grow his tail again. He's cutting away the cells that make the transformation. Like Saegar, he'll have to live on land."

"Yes. I told you I was choosing exile," Joran repeated. He freed himself as he spoke, and his tail sagged, lifeless and still trapped, against the rocks. His legs were white and thin, and he moved them like a frog, in a jerky motion, as he began to swim upward and away.

"If I'd focused, years ago, on getting rid of you, Loucan..." he signed. "But I underestimated you. I never thought you'd unite the mer the way you have. I thought that anyone who'd lived as long on land as you would be too weak.... My mistake. Interesting that this is the way I'll have to pay for it, living there, too."

"You could go after him, Loucan," Lass said. "He's powerless now."

She ran her fingers along Loucan's strong arm, certain that he must regret the way Joran had taken his destiny into his own hands. For Loucan's sake, she had begun to crave a more decisive victory, too. In her peripheral vision, she saw Carrag and the rest of the patrol approaching, and then Ben and Kai. Ben was taking pictures with his high-tech underwater camera, of Joran's thin, ungainly body swimming frantically toward the ocean's surface and away over the battle-scarred reefs.

"Yes, he's powerless," Loucan agreed. "And everyone can see it. Which is why I'm not going to go after him. Let him choose a life of exile among the land-dwellers he despises. I've got something more important to do, Lass. With you."

He turned to her, and answered the concern in her touch by holding her in his arms. Drifting with him toward the surface of the water, Lass was barely aware of the crowds of mer people beginning to gather at a respectful distance around them.

"What is more important to you than Pacifica, Loucan?" she asked him urgently. "This is a decisive moment. Whatever you have to say to me can wait."

She traced her fingers across his lips, sealing the promise of her new patience.

But Loucan shook his head, his blue eyes bright and sure. "It's waited long enough. And you're right. This is a decisive moment. In Pacifica's history, but more importantly in ours."

They reached the surface and came up into the strong sunlight. It danced on the water and made the whitecaps, stirred up by the tropical breeze, look as clean as snow. A dark spot in the distance might have been Joran's head, bobbing above the water, or it might have been a piece of driftwood.

"I love you, Lass," Loucan said. "I wouldn't blame you if you threw the words back in my face, but I have to say them. I love you. I should have understood how I felt, and told you on the boat. I shouldn't have needed the sickening fear I felt today when I realized Joran had you. You've been angry at my priorities—"

"Not anymore. I owe it to Joran, just as you do, Loucan, that I'm seeing the truth more clearly now." She brushed the dark, wet strands of his hair back from his strong forehead and stroked his smooth brown skin. "He could talk about killing me and making me his wife in the same breath. It was—" she shook her head "—crazy. All you've ever shown me was respect and honesty and care. I love you so much."

"And I love you. More than I ever dreamed possible."

It was a very private confession. Loucan's arms crushed Lass against his chest, and she never wanted him to let her go. It didn't matter where they were. Here in Pacifica, as joint rulers over a peaceful nation. Wandering the ocean in his boat, or running her little tearoom with its views of mountains and sea.

"I want to be with you forever, as your wife," she whispered, and he kissed her while the words were still on her lips.

Around them, gathering in greater numbers every second, the mer people cheered. Lass blinked and laughed, then pillowed her head against Loucan's chest as he slowly turned in the water and waved to the growing crowd. It was a regal gesture, but his other arm, around Lass's waist, was purely the arm of a lover, caressing her. The crowd cheered again, and there were no dissenting voices.

Ben had his camera ready once more, and his diving mask pulled back. Kai was grinning beside him as he lifted the viewfinder to his eye.

"Since you don't have wedding pictures," he said, "you can have these instead."

Epilogue

"Baby pictures," Loucan said to Lass.

He flung a packet of photos onto the table in the galley of the *Ondina,* and Lass stretched her hand out for them eagerly. "Oh, I was *hoping* they would have arrived! Kai said she would send them."

Loucan had set up a post office box here to help her communicate more easily with her siblings in the United States. He and Lass had reached his boat last night. It was moored at a marina on one of Hawaii's quieter islands, and they'd taken longer than usual to make the swim here, since Lass's pregnancy had begun to slow her down. She was still feeling very tired, and they would take a few days to rest before flying to California to see the newest member of the Pacifican royal clan, and his proud parents, Kai and Ben.

The photos of baby Kean—pronounced Key-ahn, and named for their father, Okeana—whetted Lass's appetite in a dangerous way, and she told her husband, "You know, I think we could fly out tomorrow, really. I'm feeling fine now."

"I picked up the airline tickets, and our flight is three days away," he answered, in a tone she'd learned to recognize—and accept. It was a tone that said, *I'm right about this, and if we're both patient, you'll realize the fact.*

She sighed. "Okay."

"Lass, if you can tell me you don't need a two-hour nap each day, and that you didn't get sick every time you tried to eat on the journey here, I'll change the tickets."

But she did need the nap, and she had gotten sick, trying to eat while on the move. Hardly surprising, since two mer doctors had recently confirmed her own intuition that she was carrying twins. Her due date was still nearly six months away, and they planned to be safely back in Pacifica by then, so that she could give birth underwater, in a special heated pool.

After visiting California, where they would also meet up with Phoebe, Kevin, Saegar, Beth and Ben, they would fly to Australia to finalize the sale of Lass's property to Susie and Rob.

"Did it occur to you that Susie almost guessed, at our wedding, that there was something a little unusual about us?" Loucan asked as he put away the baby pictures.

"You want to tell them, don't you?" Lass guessed.

"I want to show them. I've believed since Cody's death that this is the way we have to handle it—opening up first to the people we trust. With peace in Pacifica now, the time has come to start the experiment."

Lass thought of Susie's warm brown eyes and

Rob's thoughtful manner. She remembered their rapport with her horses, and saw in her mind the bird-attracting shrubs Rob had begun to plant in her garden. "We've got to recognize our kinship to all creatures," Rob had said to her once, in his shy, quiet way. "We shouldn't do anything to drive them away."

"Yes," she answered Loucan. "I think you're right about opening up to people we trust. And even if I didn't think you were right about that and most things, everyone else in Pacifica does. There's been no sign at all that peace won't hold." She thought back on their swim across the coral reefs a few days ago. "Even the coral on the damaged sections of reef is starting to regenerate. Didn't you think so?"

"In some places," Loucan said. "It'll take a while to look the way it used to."

"Do you think Joran reached inhabited land safely?"

This time, she saw the way her husband hesitated. "There've been some rumors recently," he said. "A sighting in Fiji, and one a few weeks later in New Zealand."

"Who saw him?"

"First Carrag and Nacre, on their honeymoon. And then another long-time supporter of mine who's wandering the world the way I once did."

"You didn't tell me. You thought it would upset me," she guessed.

"Only because—"

"I might be pregnant, Loucan—"

"With twins," he interjected, as if it made a difference.

''—but that doesn't change who I am. Don't you dare think you can—'' She stopped abruptly.

He was laughing. Before she could harness her indignation into the proud, angry speech she wanted to make, he pulled her to her feet and into his arms.

''Give me a break,'' he said softly. He brushed his mouth across hers. Her lips parted all by themselves, with her familiar need to taste him and return his kiss. ''Is it wrong to treat you as if you're precious? Ben treated Kai like glass when she was pregnant. That was how we guessed, remember? The day they arrived in Pacifica, after the whole mess with Joran was over? You're *so* precious to me, Lass. You know that. So give me a break, and let me pamper you, the way I want to.''

''Oh, Loucan...'' She laughed, too, even while tears filled her eyes.

''Just don't tell anyone, okay? Might not be good for the whole of Pacifica to know that their king is totally nuts about his queen.''

''Loucan, they realized that months ago,'' Lass told him happily. She realized it herself, but it was always nice to hear him say it.

''Yeah, I guess they did,'' he answered. ''Hey, are you ready to take your afternoon nap, by any chance?''

''Why do I suspect it's not going to be all that restful today, King Loucan?''

''Can't imagine, Queen Thalassa.''

He carried her to the newly refitted cabin, with its brand-new queen-size bed, and the rest of the afternoon evaporated in a haze of delight, which they both knew would last in their hearts forever.

* * * * *

Silhouette
SPECIAL EDITION™
&
SILHOUETTE Romance®
present a new series about the proud, passion-driven dynasty
THE COLTONS
You loved the California Coltons, now discover the Coltons of Black Arrow, Oklahoma. Comanche blood courses through their veins, but a brand-new birthright awaits them....
WHITE DOVE'S PROMISE by Stella Bagwell (7/02, SE#1478)
THE COYOTE'S CRY by Jackie Merritt (8/02, SE#1484)
WILLOW IN BLOOM by Victoria Pade (9/02, SE#1490)
THE RAVEN'S ASSIGNMENT by Kasey Michaels (9/02, SR#1613)
A COLTON FAMILY CHRISTMAS by Judy Christenberry, Linda Turner and Carolyn Zane (10/02, Silhouette Single Title)
SKY FULL OF PROMISE by Teresa Southwick (11/02, SR#1624)
THE WOLF'S SURRENDER by Sandra Steffen (12/02, SR#1630)
Look for these titles wherever Silhouette books are sold!
Silhouette®
Where love comes alive™
Visit Silhouette at www.eHarlequin.com
SSECOLT

SILHOUETTE Romance

COMING NEXT MONTH

#1624 SKY FULL OF PROMISE—Teresa Southwick
The Coltons
Dr. Dominic Rodriguez's fiancée ran out on him—and it was all Sky Colton's fault! Feeling guilty about the breakup, Sky reluctantly posed as Dom's finacée to calm his frazzled mother. But would their pretend engagement lead to a real marriage proposal?

#1625 HIS BEST FRIEND'S BRIDE—Jodi O'Donnell
Bridgewater Bachelors
Born in the same hospital on the same day, Julia Sennett, Griff Corbin and Reb Farley were best friends—until romance strained their bonds. Engaged to Reb, Julia questioned her choice in future husbands. Now Griff must choose between his childhood buddy…and the woman he loves!

#1626 STRANDED WITH SANTA—Janet Tronstad
Wealthy, successful rodeo cowboy Zack Lucas hated Christmas—he didn't want to be a mail-carrying Santa and he certainly didn't want to fall in love with Jenny Collins. But a brutal Montana storm left Zach snowbound on his mail route, which meant spending the holidays in Jenny's arms...!

#1627 THE BARON & THE BODYGUARD—Valerie Parv
The Carramer Legacy
Stricken with amnesia, Mathiaz de Marigny didn't remember telling his beautiful bodyguard that he loved her—or that she had refused him. Now Jacinta Newnham vowed a new start between them. But what would happen when the truth surrounding Mathiaz's accident—and Jacinta's connection to it—surfaced?

#1628 HER LAST CHANCE—DeAnna Talcott
Soulmates
Looking for a spirited filly with unicorn blood, foreign heiress Mallory Chevalle found no-nonsense horse breeder Chase Wells. According to legend, his special horse could heal her ailing father and restore harmony to her homeland. But could a love-smitten Mallory heal Chase's wounded heart?

#1629 CHRISTMAS DUE DATE—Moyra Tarling
Mac Kingston was a loner who hadn't counted on sharing the holidays—or his inheritance—with very beautiful, very wary and very pregnant Eve Darling. But when she realized she'd found the perfect father—and husband!—could she convince Mac?

SRCNM1002